BOOK CHALLENGE WINNER

SLAM DUNK
INTO REALITY

D1147322

SLAM DUNK
INTO REALITY

Kim Sandy

CHRISTIAN FOCUS PUBLICATIONS

© 1999 Kim Sandy
ISBN 1-85792-162-3
First published 1996
Reprinted 1999

Published by Christian Focus Publications
Geanies House, Fearn, Ross-shire
IV20 1TW, Scotland, Great Britain

Cover design by Donna Macleod
Cover illustration by Graham Kennedy, Allied Artists

Printed and bound in Great Britain by
Cox & Wyman Ltd, Reading, Berks

Contents

Chapter 1

It just wasn't fair! Andrew Price was going on a Wildlife Safari in Kenya for his holidays. Leroy and Anthony Brown were going to Jamaica. Marcus Osbourne was going to Spain and Jonathan Wright was going to Portugal. For them there would be an amazing aeroplane journey across the skies. For them there would be thrills and adventures, exciting places and golden beaches. For them the school holidays would be the time of their lives with memories to treasure and fantastic photographs to look back on. For Ben Carpenter, the six-weeks' holidays would be spent in a rented cottage named 'Village Heights,' situated in a deserted part of a sleepy village called Westly Point, somewhere along the Cornish coast. It would probably rain every day and the youngest person to hang around with would be an 89-year-old Granddad.

'Why can't we go to Florida?' Ben asked (for the hundredth time that week).

'You know why,' his father said wearily.

'Actually I don't know why. I can't see why I should be dragged off to Snooze Cottage in the middle of nowhere. What am I going to do stuck out there?' Ben's nose creased in anger. His top lip began to curl up. He knew he was trying his parent's patience but this was his last attempt at changing their minds before tomorrow when they would set off for the Valley of Boredom.

'I want to go to Disney World.'

'Oh no, here we go again, just turned 14-years-old and he's moaning about Disney World again. I knew he never really got over his crush on Snow White,' said Ben's father.

Ben didn't appreciate the humour. 'Oh very funny,' he said in his most sarcastic voice. 'Actually, I want to go to the Epcot Centre. It's an experimental prototype community of tomorrow, a cross between a science museum and a theme park,' he protested, with a look that said, 'so there!'

'Oh, well grab your coats everyone, let's go right now,' said his father.

Ben was annoyed. His father always made a big joke out of everything but he wouldn't give up easily.

'Well? Why can't we go?'

Ben's mother sighed and his father shook his head slowly, opened up his newspaper and began to read. This was his way of saying that the subject was closed, but Ben was desperate.

'Well? Why do we have to go to 'Village Lows'? We might as well stay here because there's nothing for me out there. I don't want to go!'

'How many times to we have to tell you?' his mother began, her voice pleading. 'I need peace and quiet to finish the book that I'm writing and ever since your Dad lost his job money has been tight for us. We're lucky to be having a holiday at all. We got the cottage at a real bargain price.'

'Yeah, that's because nobody in their right minds would

want to go there,' said Ben. He knew that he was losing the battle.

Putting down his paper Dan looked directly at his son, 'Come on Ben, we'll have a great time. We can go fishing. Just the two of us. No women allowed.'

'Boring,' sang Ben in a monotonous tone.

'We can go for walks,' his father continued.

'Boring,' Ben rolled his eyes toward the ceiling and folded his arms in front of his chest.

'We can take your basketball and you can teach me how to do a New York Spin or whatever that new move you learnt is called.'

'Boring.'

'We can take your cricket bat and I can show you my fantastic batting technique.'

'Mega boring,' said Ben. He was still staring moodily at the ceiling waiting for his father to think up another activity but his Dad had given up.

'I'm not going to argue with you, Benjamin. We are going to the cottage and we will have a peaceful, family holiday whether you like it or not.'

'Well I don't like it!' Ben shouted. 'I don't like it one little bit!'

'Don't you Ben? I'd never have guessed,' said his father trying not to smirk at his own wit.

'Oh go on then, laugh at me,' Ben began, his anger boiling over. 'You'll be sorry when I have a heart attack and die of boredom - then you'll wish you had taken me to Florida.' Slamming the door hard, Ben headed for his bedroom, going up the stairs two at a time and muttering angrily to himself.

'Oh Dan, he will be all right won't he?' His mother was concerned.

'Of course he will, Claire,' came the reply. 'He'll have a fantastic time, just you wait and see.'

Upstairs Ben grumbled quietly to himself. 'This is going to be the worst six weeks of my life. When I have kids I'll take them to Florida twice a year.'

Chapter 2

'Mum can I take my computer?'

It was Saturday. It was 6 am and Benjamin's father was loading suitcases into the boot of their car. His mother was carrying out an inspection of the house.

'Okay, so I've checked the gas, the electricity is switched off, the back door is bolted - did you close the window in your room, Ben?'

'Yes, Mum,' Ben answered. 'Mum, can I take my computer?'

'Oh Ben, no you can't. Sorry, love,' said his mother.

'Why can't I? You're taking yours. Oh please, Mum!' said Benjamin. His voice took on a begging tone that sometimes worked with his mother.

'No, darling. Sorry,' she said firmly. Ben knew she wouldn't change her mind. 'Mine's a lap-top, it's supposed to be transported around - yours isn't and besides, there's better things for you to be doing than sitting around playing computer games all day.'

'But, Mum,' Benjamin tried, 'Anthony just lent me his new game. It's the latest one on the market and it's brilliant. I've only played it once so far.'

Benjamin's father entered and picked up a suitcase that was standing in the middle of the room.

'Are we moaning about Florida again?'

'No,' said Ben's mother fatigued, 'he wants to take his computer.'

'I've got a new game to play. It'll keep me occupied while we're on holiday.'

'Sorry Ben,' said his father, 'the car's almost full. We might even have to leave your mum behind,' Dan winked at his wife who laughed in surprise.

'Oi, you. What a cheek! You just try leaving me behind,' she said. Her face lit up with happiness. She was excited about the holiday and had been looking forward to it for ages. Seeing how cheerful she looked, made Ben feel guilty about being such a wet blanket all the time, but he was still cross. They should have considered him when they booked the holiday. In Florida they had basketball courts on every corner and the kids in the States played all day long. Ben could have really improved his game. They didn't care if he went stir-crazy stuck out in the sticks. With a flash of inspiration Ben said, 'Hey Dad, do you think they'll have Sky TV at the cottage?' There was an all-day sports channel on Sky and Ben was hoping to see some basketball matches.

Dan Carpenter hesitated. He looked carefully at his wife. This was the first sign of enthusiasm Ben had shown for weeks and neither parent wanted to throw cold water on it.

'Well Ben, it didn't say anything about Sky TV in the brochure - but that doesn't mean they won't have it. They might have Cable. We'll have to wait and see; you never know, you might be lucky.'

Ben could tell by his father's careful answer that there was probably very little chance of finding Sky TV in the cottage.

'Yeah, sure Dad, and I'm Michael Jordan, Michael Jackson and Michael Mouse rolled into one,' said Ben sarcastically.

It was a long journey to the cottage. Ben sat moodily in the back seat of the car. Whenever his parents tried to make conversation with him, he pretended to be asleep. He must have actually drifted off for real at some point because before he knew it his mother was gently shaking his arm.

'We're here, Ben, come and see the cottage. It's breathtaking.'

Benjamin got out of the car and stretched his long limbs. His mother was already taking photographs. She had that funny look on her face again, like a little girl on Christmas morning. Seeing Ben awake, his father yelled, 'Hey, Ben, the boot's open, grab a case and bring it inside will you.'

Lifting two heavy cases, Ben lugged them inside.

The cottage was everything he had feared it would be. A white building with a thick thatched roof. Around the front door tied to a trellis was a rambling rose bush, its deep crimson petals and glossy green leaves stood out like a blaze of colour against the whiteness of the cottage walls.

'Boring,' murmured Ben to himself as he dropped the suitcases on the floor inside.

'Isn't it adorable!' His mother gasped as they looked around the place that was to be their home for the next 42 days. 'That's over one thousand hours,' thought Benjamin miserably to himself.

'I love the heavy wooden beams on the walls and the ceiling... and oh, look an open fire,' his mother was enthralled by the place and had clearly fallen in love with it; they'd be lucky if they could get her to go home again. 'This is the perfect place for me to work, it's so peaceful, so homely, so...' she searched for words, 'so inspiring,' she said finally.

'So dull, so dead,' said Benjamin under his breath. He knew there was no chance of finding Sky TV here. In fact just finding a television would be a miracle. This place didn't even look as though it had electricity.

'Let's look upstairs,' said Ben's mother. Together the three of them climbed the wooden staircase to explore the upper part of the cottage. Ben's parents were thrilled with the ancient four-poster bed that was in their room and they liked the old-fashioned pitcher jug and wash bowl that sat on the antique dressing table. Curious to see what his room was like but not wanting to show too much enthusiasm, Ben sneaked quietly away to investigate.

The room was quite ordinary really with a bed, a wardrobe, a chest of drawers and an old rocking chair in it. Secretly Ben was rather pleased with the rocking chair and sat on it straight away. It creaked heavily as Ben rocked it backwards and forwards. Throwing his weight into the back of the chair, he rocked it faster and faster until it suddenly propelled him out of the seat and on to the floor.

Landing with a thud in the centre of the room he got up quickly and was thankful that his parents hadn't seen him, they would have laughed until they cried. The large window in his room didn't have any nets or curtains, there was nothing to obscure the amazing view outside. Walking to the window Ben could see miles and miles of open countryside looking back at him. The amazing rolling green scenery and majestic hills made Ben wish he was a better artist. He would love to paint this scene but he could never do it justice. From here he could see the beach, it was about a mile away and he was already looking forward to trekking across the countryside to get a closer look at it. At least it wouldn't be packed with people. Ben couldn't see another cottage around for miles, they were completely isolated.

'What do you think of the place?' his father asked. He was standing in the doorway of Ben's room. Behind him Ben could see his mother.

'You do like it, don't you, Ben?' asked his mother. She sounded so concerned that Ben decided he would make the effort to stop moaning.

'Yeah, it's boss,' said Ben. He grinned at his parents.

'I think, my dear, that means he likes it,' explained Dan to his wife.

Chapter 3

On Sunday morning the Carpenters climbed into their car and drove along quiet country lanes in search of a shop.

'There must be one somewhere,' said Claire, 'how do people get milk and bread around here?'

'What people?' asked Ben, with a wry smile on his face.

Dan looked into his rear view mirror and smiled back at his son who was sprawled on the back seat of the car. 'True,' he said laughing. 'Can't say I've seen anyone else since we arrived.'

'LOOK OUT!' Ben's mother screamed. His father slammed hard on the brakes and the car screeched to halt. Standing just centimetres in front of the car was an old woman.

'Oh dear, oh dearie me,' she said when Ben's father leapt out to see if she was all right. 'You nearly gave me heart failure.'

'I'm terribly sorry,' said Dan, 'I took my eyes off the road for a split second... I'm really sorry. You're not hurt are you?'

'No dear, no bones broken,' the old lady said kindly.

'You must be on holiday here, are you staying at Village Heights?'

'Yes, we are, as it happens. We'll be there for six weeks.'

'That's nice for you.'

'Yes,' said Dan, 'I wonder if you could tell us where the nearest shop is?'

'Oh you'll have to be going into the village for shops. Just stay on this road, it's a good five miles, mind you, but you can't miss it.'

'Thank you very much,' said Dan, 'and I'm really sorry for giving you a scare. I hope you'll be all right.'

'Don't you worry, I'm fine. Tell you what, if you get the chance take the next left and you'll see our church. You'd be more than welcome. There's lots of people there if you get lonely and there's plenty of youngsters for your lad to mix with.'

Dan smiled politely, 'Thank you, we'll bear that in mind.' He got back into the car and they waved at the lady as they drove past.

'Please, please, please tell me that we won't be going to 'Old Mother Hubbard's' church, said Ben.

'Oh, there's no danger of that, love,' said his mother, and, singing *Ten Green Bottles*, they drove on to the shops.

*   *   *   *   *

Compared to the busy shopping centre in the town where Ben lived, the village was tiny. A few shops were scattered around a large green circle of grass with a duck pond in the middle. There was a post office, a general store, a craft shop that sold wool and embroidery threads, an antique store and a little tea shop. Dan and Claire headed

17

straight for the antique shop and spent ages looking at a collection of antique toys. The shop reeked of everything that was old and musty. It was of no interest whatsoever to Ben so he stepped outside and breathed deeply of the fresh air. He was certain he could hear the distinctive bouncing of a basketball, it sounded quite close.

Following the noise to behind the shop, he was amazed to see three boys shooting ball. They were playing on an old tennis court that had been converted for basketball. Quality rims had been put up, outdoor ones with chain nets that clinked impressively whenever a basket was scored. Ben watched for a while. These guys could play! The boys were about the same age as Ben, perhaps slightly older, but where on earth did they learn how to play B Ball like that? One boy was particularly outstanding. Ben watched him drive the ball past one defender, fake the other and then leap into the air to execute a perfect hook shot.

'Nice basket!' Ben clapped his hands slowly with admiration.

'Thanks,' said the boy, 'Wanna play?'

Ben didn't need asking twice. 'Sure,' he said and ran on to the court.

'Let's play two-on-two,' said the boy, 'you be on my side, I'm Jake, this is Ricky and this is Joe,' he said, pointing to his friends.

'I'm Ben.' He took the ball and bounced it a few times.

'Why don't you take a few warm up shots and then we'll get the game started,' said Jake.

Stepping up to the free throw line, Ben bounced the ball twice before taking his shot. It hit the rim and rebounded away. Ricky passed the ball back and Ben tried again but this time the ball missed the hoop entirely. He cringed with embarrassment. His third attempt was worse still. 'I'm a bit rusty,' Ben lied, 'I haven't played for a while.'

'Try bending your knees when you throw and flick your wrist when you release the ball,' said Jake. He took the ball and demonstrated the technique. It sunk convincingly into the net. Grabbing the ball, Ben did what Jake had done. Bending his knees he sprung up and took his shot. As he released the ball he flicked his wrist down the way Jake had. With a swish the ball cut the net. There was no way Ben could conceal the huge grin on his face.

'All right!' Jake smiled, ' the match is on.'

Ben turned to the sound of enthusiastic clapping coming from behind him. His parents were watching.

'Excellent goal,' his father shouted.

Ben walked quickly over to his parents. 'It's not a goal, it's a basket,' he said quietly.

'Oh, pardon me!' said Dan.

'Well done, Ben! We knew you were interested in basketball but we didn't know you were that good,' said his mother.

Ben was glad they didn't see his first three attempts at the basket. 'Listen, Mum, Dad, they want me to play a game with them, is it okay if I stay here for a while?'

'Of course you can,' his mother replied, 'we'll just go and have some scones at the tea shop and meet you back here in about half an hour.'

'Excellent! Thanks.' Ben ran back to the game and within seconds was involved in a friendly match. Perhaps this holiday wouldn't be so bad after all.

Fifteen minutes later Jake and Ben were winning 8 - 4. Ben couldn't believe how good his shooting was now.

He just couldn't miss. Suddenly Jake stopped. 'What time is it?'

Joe looked at his watch. 'It's quarter to eleven - we're going to be late!'

'Sorry, Ben, we've got to go,' Jake said.

'Where are you going?' Ben was wondering if he could tag along.

'We're going to church,' said Jake, 'Want to come?'

The other boys added their voices, 'Yeah, come, Ben, you'll like it.'

'What!' Ben laughed. 'You're kidding right? You're not really going to church are you. Come on, guys, get real.'

The boys looked offended. 'What's wrong with church?' Jake asked.

'Well, nothing, if you're about 85 and haven't got anything better to do,' said Ben.

'You're wrong, Ben.' Jake shook his head. 'Why don't you come with us, see for yourself.'

'No way!' Ben suddenly burst into laughter. 'This is a joke right? Okay you got me, where's Jeremy Beadle?'

'Sorry, Ben,' said Ricky, 'we are going to church.'

'Yeah and if we don't go now we're going to be late,' said Jake. 'See you around sometime, Ben,' he shouted as they ran away.

Ben sat angrily on the court. He couldn't even shoot some hoops on his own - Jake had taken the ball. Surely they weren't really going to church, they seemed like ordinary guys. Disappointed he got up and went to find his parents.

The tea shop was rather small but filled with the delicious smells of home-baking. There were several round tables scattered about, each covered with a pretty yellow and white checked table cloth. On each table sat a tiny vase bursting with delightfully fragrant flowers. Ben saw his parents sitting by the window.

'Ah, Benjamin, that was quick,' said his father. 'Come and have some of these scrumptious scones.' He patted the chair next to him indicating that Ben should sit there.

'Finished your game already?' His mother asked.

'Yeah, you'll never guess where they've all rushed off to,' Ben's voice was full of incredulity.

'Don't tell me,' said his father, 'the Chicago Bulls are three men short and they've been drafted in? Have a scone.'

'Nope. They've gone to church,' said Ben flatly.

'Oh well, it take's all sorts to make a world go round,' said his mother consoling him.

'Yeah, I know, but they looked so normal.'

'Well, I know one thing that's not normal,' said Dan, 'these scones... they're exquisite. Have one, Ben.'

'Dad,' said Ben.

'What?' Dan replied with his mouth full.

'Will you please stop going on about scones.'

Chapter 4

On Monday Ben found an old bicycle in the shed at the bottom of the cottage garden. He thought about using it to cycle down to the village and see if Jake, Ricky and Joe were playing basketball again, but he decided not to bother. He still hadn't quite forgiven them for dashing off, just to go to church. He decided to hike down to the coast and eat sandwiches beside the sea. His mother made him a packed lunch, popped it into Ben's rucksack and then settled down at her computer to work on her book. Ben's father was relaxing in the garden, reading a new spy novel.

'Make sure you're back for tea,' said his mother. 'We're having spaghetti bolognaise.'

Ben decided that he would definitely not be late back. 'Spag Bol' was his favourite.

The beach turned out to be a mixture of pebbles and shingle but Ben didn't mind. He loved the crunching sound beneath his feet as he trekked his way across the stones. The sea lapped peacefully up to the shore, the gentle sound of waves spilling over the pebbles was calming. Ben took a deep breath, the air was so clean he felt almost light-headed. It was invigorating, a mixture of sea breeze and country atmosphere.

Above him gulls flew aimlessly in circles, screeching loudly. Their sounds, ironically, added to the tranquillity of the beach. Climbing up on to a large rock, Ben pulled his rucksack off his back and took out the food that his mother had prepared. She had packed two cold chicken drumsticks and a buttered roll. There was also a packet of crisps, three chocolate biscuits and a can of fizzy orange. Delighted with this Ben tucked greedily into his lunch, beginning with a drumstick.

The tide was beginning to go out. Ben finished eating and packed his empty lunch box back into his rucksack. He decided to skim a few stones over the water before heading back to the cottage. He searched for smooth flat stones that would skip over the water well. When he had found a handful he began skilfully throwing them at such an angle that they bounced merrily over the water, before sinking with a resounding plop. Ben's best attempt bounced five times. Determined to beat his own record he searched for better stones. He had just filled the pockets of his jeans with pebbles when he noticed something glittering on the shore. It wasn't far away and he could easily have run over to see what it was but he hesitated.

Ben took two steps towards the object. Bright silver light flashed from it like a mirror when it catches the sun. Maybe it was a mirror? Cautiously, Ben walked toward it. It was a peculiar shaped stone, no larger than Ben's hand but shaped almost like a crystal. His heart was pounding. Filled with a sense of danger and exhilaration Ben reached down to touch it. What was this? Where did it come from? Maybe it was worth a lot of money, or perhaps he would become famous for discovering it.

As his finger made contact with the stone, it immediately stopped flashing. Ben wondered for a moment if he had imagined it all. Maybe the light was playing tricks on him. Maybe he had been out in the fresh air too long. Maybe he was losing his marbles. Holding the stone up in front of his face, Ben studied its striking form. It was beautiful. It looked like it had been carefully chiselled by a master craftsman. His mother would probably like to use it as a paper weight. Twisting the stone in the sunlight he marvelled at it until he noticed that the sky was growing quite dark. It got darker and darker with terrifying speed. It was completely black now. Ben couldn't see anything around him at all. Now he was scared, very scared.

'What's going on?' he cried out into the blackness. He could hear the waves rising up and crashing angrily against the shore. The wind moaned menacingly and whipped up the sand. Ben began to run, but the force of the wind was too strong. Whatever direction he chose the wind was there, like a force field, pushing him back, bullying him to stay where he was. In his frenzied attempts to escape, Ben tripped and fell heavily on to the pebbles. 'Stop! Please!' he screamed, lying with his face against the cold stones. His knee hurt and he couldn't get up. 'I'm going to die,' he thought, 'the waves will reach me and I'll drown.'

'Help me!'

The sky instantly flashed with the most amazing blinding white light. Ben squinted, covering his eyes with his forearm. The stone in his hand had miraculously changed. Now it appeared to be made of glass, a pure white light radiated from it and sparks of colour, mostly greens and purples, were leaping into the air and filling the sky. The colours swirled so fast that Ben felt dizzy. He had to get rid of the stone. He tried throwing it but it was fixed to his hand. Desperately he tried shaking it loose but it was impossible. With horror Ben felt himself rising from the ground, he struggled against it but was powerless to prevent himself from being drawn into the madness of whirling colour. His body was now a part of it, spinning round and round, faster and faster. His mouth opened and Ben knew he was screaming but he could hear nothing, other than the sound of the wind as it spun him in all directions.

He must have passed out then because when he awoke he was lying on a dusty road. A small child was poking him with a stick.

'Where am I?' Ben asked. He wasn't sure what had happened, hopefully it was all a dream. The child didn't answer but continued to poke him.

'Cut it out, will you!' Ben said. He stood up and rubbed his face, he was confused. This morning he was wearing a red T-shirt, a pair of jeans and a pair of the latest basketball trainers. Now he was wearing a dress!

'Man, is this some kind of sick joke or what?' Ben looked at his feet. He was wearing sandals. He groaned miserably.

The small child took Ben's hand and clutched it.

'Where hast thou been!' said a voice behind Ben.

He turned quickly to find himself face to face with a boy of about his own age.

The boy's face dropped when he looked into Ben's eyes. 'I am mistaken. My friend is missing. His parents are filled with grief and are seeking him.' Turning to the small child, the boy said, 'It is not him, Daniel. This is a stranger.'

The child looked up at Ben and realising that this was not who he had thought it was, suddenly let go of Ben's hand.

'Do I look like this missing boy, then?' Ben asked, intrigued.

'No, but he was wearing a brown tunic like thine.'

Ben looked down at his daft dress and cringed again.

'Who art thou?' the boy asked.

'What?' Ben wasn't sure what he meant.

'Who art thou?' the boy repeated. 'What is thy name?'

'Me? Oh, I'm erm... Benjamin, but you can call me Ben.'

Ben couldn't help noticing that the boy was wearing a dress too and he had this funny way of talking.

'I'm Zachariah, but thou canst call me Zach,' said the boy. 'This is my brother, Daniel.' He nodded at the small child.

A group of about four men and three women, suddenly rushed over to them. Anxiety was written all over their faces.

'Hast thou seen him, Zachariah?' one of the men asked Zach.

'No, Father.' Zach bowed his head. He seemed quite worried himself.

'We shall go back to the town. Surely he must be there,' one of the men said.

The group of adults rushed away. Ben could hear one of the women crying.

Daniel suddenly ran to catch up with his father. Zach turned to Ben. 'Dost thou live in the town?' he asked.

'Yeah, I come from a town,' Ben replied.

'Walk back with us, then, Ben, if it pleases thee.'

Ben was still scared. He didn't have a clue what was

going on or where he was but he was grateful for a friendly face and someone to walk with. 'Yeah, it pleases thee, erm, I mean me,' Ben said.

Chapter 5

The town was crowded. Ben had never seen so many people, or for that matter, so many donkeys. Kids were running riot, chickens were clucking and flapping and getting in everyone's way. Ben stopped to watch a large man trying to get on a tiny donkey but the donkey was having none of it. Every time the man got on, the donkey bucked him off again. Ben found this rather amusing but when he turned around he realised that he was lost.

Ben wandered around, wondering exactly where he was. A sudden noise coming from inside a building, attracted his attention and cautiously he entered the open front door. A group of elderly looking men with long beards and fancy looking robes were sitting around a young boy. One of the men said something to him and everyone was silent waiting for his reply.

'Truly astonishing. His knowledge of scripture is amazing,' said one of the men.

'So much knowledge for such a little Rabbi!' said another.

Ben looked at the boy. He was saying something else now and the men were all listening with raised eyebrows.

Every so often they would nod or murmur their agreement. Ben liked this boy. He certainly knew his stuff but he didn't seem like some of those brain-boxes at school. What a pity he had such poor taste in clothing - his brown dress was almost as bad as Ben's.

Hey! This must be the missing boy! One of the men brought some food and placed it in front of the boy who began to eat. Ben wandered outside the building. Should he try and find Zach and let him know that he had found his friend. Before he could decide, Ben saw a man and woman marching straight for the building. Rushing back inside, Ben coughed loudly, trying to get the boy's attention. He wanted to warn him that there could be big trouble heading his way any second now, but it was too late.

The woman ran up to the boy and grabbed him by the shoulders. Tears were streaming down her face. 'Son, why hast thou done this to us? Behold thy father and I have sought thee, sorrowing.'

The whole place was silent. The boy looked calm though. Ben would have launched himself into a thousand excuses by now. But the boy stayed quiet.

'Why?' the woman repeated. 'We knew not what had become of thee!'

The elderly men were looking intensely at the boy, everyone was but then the boy said, 'How is it that ye have sought me? Didst ye not know that I would be in my Father's house?'

The old men immediately started murmuring again but the woman looked confused. The boy got up, waved goodbye to the men and left the building, with the woman.

Now what on earth was all that about? Ben wondered as he followed behind them.

'Oh no!' Ben moaned when the sky suddenly went white. Everything had disappeared. The wind was howling and he was being raised from the ground, tossed into the air, and once again, spinning in a mist of circling colours. Strange sounds engulfed him, and the voice of the boy... 'Didst ye not know I would be in my Father's house...'

*   *   *   *   *

'Benjamin Carpenter, what on earth are you doing sleeping on the doorstep? I was just coming to look for you.' The voice sounded warm and familiar.

'Dad?'

'Yes, Ben.'

'Oh, Dad,' said Ben throwing his arms around his father. 'It is so good to see thee!'

Chapter 6

After a particularly delicious meal, of which Ben had two huge helpings, he went up to his room. Standing by the window, he gazed out at the sea. What happened out there today? Did he dream it? How did he get back to the cottage, dressed in his jeans and trainers again? Something weird was going on, something sinister, something frightening. Somehow, some way, Ben had been transported to another land where there were strange people and strange happenings.

'Sucked up into the sky? Get real, Benjamin,' he said aloud to himself and yet he knew that there was no way he could have made it all up. It was far too way out - even for Ben's lively imagination.

Rushing downstairs Ben asked his mother for some paper and a pen.

'What are you going to write?' she asked him, curious that Ben should want to be writing while on holiday.

'Erm, well, I have to write an essay for our English class and I thought I might as well get a head start and do it now,' Ben answered. It was half true. He did have to write an essay for English but that wasn't what he was going to write now. Right now Ben wanted to make a record of everything that happened today He didn't want to forget a single detail.

An hour later, Benjamin had finished writing. He flexed his fingers several times and wriggled his wrist. So this was what writer's cramp felt like. He hid his work under his bed, it was so bizarre, like the writings of a madman, but it happened. It definitely happened. Ben decided that he must never go back to the sea again, it was far too dangerous. Tired and exhausted he put on his pyjamas and went downstairs to say goodnight to his parents.

'You look all in,' Dan said when he saw his son.

'Yeah, I'm really tired. I'm gonna hit the sack now,' said Ben.

He was still disturbed by thoughts of the boy, the old men with their long beards, and the swirling colours but he would worry about it tomorrow. For now all he wanted to do was to sleep.

'Are you sure you're all right, Ben?' his mother asked. 'You're not coming down with anything are you?'

'No, I don't think so,' Ben replied. 'I'm just tired.'

'Okay, you get off to bed then,' she said kissing him on the forehead.

His father patted him on the legs as he walked past. 'Goodnight, son,' he said.

'Night, Dad, Night, Mum. I, er... I erm... I love you guys.' Ben went quickly up to his room.

Claire raised her eyebrows at Dan. 'He hasn't said, "I love you" since he was seven years old.'

Dan smiled. 'See, this holiday is just what he needed.'

Upstairs, Benjamin flopped onto his bed. His head sunk blissfully into his pillow and within seconds he was asleep.

Chapter 7

How could he casually mention the strange events at the beach to his parents? He could imagine his father roaring with laughter. His mother would stifle little giggles. They'd say he'd spent too many hours playing computer games or he must have been hit on the head by a basketball.

Staying close to the safety of the cottage and the security of his parents, Ben filled his time cleaning up the old bike that he had found. He played cards with his father and lazed out in the sun, but already he was beginning to feel tempted to return to the sea. Lying awake at night, Ben could hear the distant lapping of the waves and would feel irresistibly drawn to them. Where was that stone now? It wasn't in his hand when he woke up on the dusty road in that extraordinary land. The allure of the unknown was calling him, waiting for him, and Ben knew that the temptation would slowly overpower him. Soon he would return - like a man hypnotised and in a trance. But he couldn't go back there. He must never go back.

Saturday morning came quickly and Ben's resistance was broken. He would go back just once more, just to see if he could find that stone again. He wouldn't touch it, he would just look at it. He would confirm to himself that he hadn't invented it all. Quickly getting dressed, Ben crept silently down the stairs. In his hand he clutched a note, it read,

'MUM, DAD,
GONE TO THE BEACH,
LOVE, BEN.'

Placing the note carefully on the dining-room table so that it could be seen, Ben shivered. Excitement filled him. The sheer terror of what might happen today sent a rush of adrenaline pumping through his veins. Taking a deep breath of anticipation he carefully opened the door of the cottage and stepped blinking into the brilliant morning sunshine.

'Hello, love, you're up then.' Ben's parents were putting things in the boot of the car.

'What... er, what's happening?' asked Ben, baffled to see his parents up and about already. He was so sure that they were still in bed.

'Thought we'd get an early start,' said his father. 'We've packed a huge picnic and a blanket.'

'What for?' asked Ben. 'Where are we going?'

'Well it's like this,' his mother began. 'I got talking to a lady in the village who said that every year people from all over these parts gather together at a place called Ravenswood where they have a sort of festival. Apparently they have a carnival, lots of fun and games, there's tons to do and see, activities for the kids, entertainments, a bazaar and a...'

'Okay Mum, I get the picture,' said Ben. 'But why

34

didn't you tell me about it before? I was just going to the beach.'

'Oh, don't worry about that, the beach isn't going anywhere for the next few weeks. We thought it would be a nice surprise for you, that's all,' said Ben's father.

'Come on,' said his mother. 'I'll make you some breakfast before we go.'

Maybe this was fate's way of intervening. Stopping him from doing anything foolish. What would happen if he was sucked up into the whirlwind of colours again and couldn't get back to reality. He mustn't allow the sea to lure him back. He must be strong. He would go to the festival and forget all about his close encounters of the freaky kind. He would throw all his energy into enjoying himself. He was victorious, the sea could not entice him today.

Chapter 8

Bursting at the seams with laughing people, the festival was alive with activity. Several people wore fancy-dress costumes and there were clowns everywhere, wearing wild and brightly coloured curly wigs, and shiny red noses. Men in enormous Teddy-bear costumes were followed by a trail of chattering children who squealed with delight whenever a teddy chased them. Someone had dressed up as Mickey Mouse and children flocked around to shake hands with him.

'Here you are Ben,' said his father. 'Who needs Disney World?' Dan put his arm around his son's shoulders and gave him a squeeze.

Mickey came over to them and shook their hands.

'Pleased to meet you, Michael Mouse,' said Dan. He grinned at Ben.

There were hundreds of stalls to look at, each one vividly decorated with bright banners, balloons and flags. Benjamin had never seen so many balloons. The whole festival was an explosion of colour, of stimulating sounds and mouth-watering smells. The air was charged with energy and music blasted from each stall. All around

Ben could hear screams of happiness from children and regular outbursts of hilarity from the adults.

The Carpenters went from stall to stall, buying, looking, and having a go at the different games. Dan played a darts game and managed to win a toy. It was a small, pink, fluffy piglet with a curly tail. He gave it to Claire who was so thrilled with it that she promptly named it Mabel and tucked it safely under her arm.

'All right Ben?' a voice said. Ben turned to see Jake standing beside him, with him were two girls.

'Hi, Jake,' said Ben. He noticed that Jake was wearing a pair of red basketball shorts and a red vest with a white number 77 on the front. One of the girls carried a basketball.

'This is Ben, the boy I told you about. The one we met in the village,' Jake said to the girls.

Ben wondered what Jake had said about him.

'This is my sister, Melanie and this is Kate,' said Jake. He pointed to each of the girls in turn.

'Hello,' said Ben wishing he could think of something witty or clever to say but hello was the best he could manage.

The girls smiled at Ben.

'Kate is Jake's girlfriend,' said Melanie. She grinned like someone who held top secret information.

'Melanie!' Jake protested.

Kate blushed and Ben laughed at Melanie's audacity.

'She's terrible, my sister... I'd steer well clear of her if I were you,' said Jake, but he was smiling at his sister.

'I'm no ordinary sister though, am I?' Melanie questioned. 'In fact I am Jake's twin sister and I'm the eldest.'

'Only by ten minutes,' Jake reminded her.

'Oh yes, but what a wonderful ten minutes it was,' Melanie teased.

'They're always like this,' said Kate laughing. 'But they love each other really.'

'We do not!' Jake and Melanie said in unison.

Ben liked them. Jake was dead lucky to have a girlfriend as nice as Kate. He liked Melanie's fun personality and bags of confidence. She was pretty too, better-looking than Jake!

'Jake and some of the other boys from our village are in the basketball tournament. Come and watch if you like,' Melanie said to Ben. 'You can help us cheer them to victory. They need all the support they can get.'

Ben was pleased Melanie had asked him. Maybe she liked him.

'It starts at 11 o'clock.' Melanie pointed to her left, 'See that big blue tent?'

'Yeah,' Ben replied.

'Well the courts are just behind there.'

'Great, thanks, I'll probably come over later.'

'See you later then,' said Jake. 'Better go and warm up now.' He waved as he walked away.

Kate and Melanie followed behind him. They were whispering something to each other and then suddenly erupted into giggles. Melanie glanced back over her shoulder and waved. Trying to act casual, Ben waved back. He suddenly remembered his parents and wondered where they had got to. He looked around for them and was surprised to see his father still playing the darts game. When Ben looked at his mother he was amused to see that Mabel the pig had now acquired six new friends.

Chapter 9

Refusing to play darts, Ben found a basketball stall where you could win a prize simply by scoring baskets.

'Come on lad,' yelled the man behind the stall. 'Score three baskets and win any toy you like.' He held out a ball to Ben.

'Go on, Ben, have a go,' his mother encouraged him.

'I'll have a go,' said Ben's father. He paid the man and was given four balls. 'Three baskets for a prize, right?' asked Dan. The man nodded.

Dan took his first shot which went way over the top of the hoop. His second fell short of the basket and his third banged heavily on the rim. 'Ohhhhh, I'm getting close,' Dan laughed.

'Come on, Dad, you've got to get one in.'

'Right, this one's going in!' Dan stared hard at the basket. Ben sniggered. The ball went too high. It didn't even come close.

'Come on, Ben, you show him how to do it,' said his mother.

'Yes, come on, let's see if you can do any better. I'll pay.' Dan gave some more money to the man who gave

Ben four balls. Remembering what Jake had taught him, Ben bent his knees. Rising up, he released the ball, flicking his wrist as he did so. It plunged into the net perfectly. His parents burst into cheers.

'Come on, son, two more to sink,' said his father.

Taking up the second ball, Ben used the same shooting technique. Soaring through the air, the ball travelled toward the net. It entered the hoop without even touching the sides.

'Oh my word!' Dan yelled. 'He's going to do it! Go on, son.'

Taking up the third ball Ben felt the pressure. He had never won anything before in his life and now all he had to do was score one more basket to win. Struggling to regain his concentration, Ben took his third shot. The ball bounced off the backboard and spun away. There was a loud groan of disappointment.

'Forget about that one,' said his father. ' Come on, one more ball left.'

Ben took up his last ball. Well, this was it. He took a long look at the hoop. He could do this. His eyes fixed on the basket. The ball floated up to the net and appeared to hover there for a split second, as if teasing them, then all at once it swooped down into the net.

'Yes!' Went up the cry from Ben and his parents. He was so excited at having succeeded that he completely forgot about his prize.

'Take your pick,' said the stall holder, pointing to a display of very large cuddly toys.

There was a huge panda wearing a red bow, an enormous old English sheepdog, several pastel coloured bears and a giant fluffy white orangutang with a daft expression on its face and long dangling arms. Ben liked it.

'I'll have the monkey please,' he said.

The stall holder lifted the enormous toy and handed it over.

'Well done, lad, I can see you've played before,' he said.

Ben held the toy as though it was a trophy. It was quite awkward to carry because of its size but Ben didn't mind. Small children pointed at his monkey and some adults even stopped to congratulate him, asking him how he had won it.

'Well, it's two o'clock now, time for some lunch,' said Ben's mother.

'Two o'clock! Oh no, I'm missing the basketball tournament. The boys I met in the village are playing and I was going to cheer them on. How can it be two o'clock already?' Ben began to panic.

'Well, I'm sure it will still be going on for hours yet. You can eat something first and then go and watch.'

'Yeah, sure,' Ben agreed reluctantly. He would have preferred to skip lunch and go straight to the tournament.

Finding a quiet space away from the flurry of activity around the stalls was not easy but when they had found a quiet spot Dan spread a large blanket down over the green grass and Claire began to unpack the picnic.

'After we've eaten, we're going to see if we can find something nice to take home as a souvenir for your Gran and Grandad,' Ben's mother told him.

'And we need to get some postcards,' said Dan. 'We'll probably wander over to see the basketball, but if not, we'll all meet back here at 5pm,' he said to his son.

'Okay, Dad, let's synchronise our watches.'

His parents laughed. They were so pleased that Ben was actually enjoying himself. It was good to see him happy.

Ben was just tucking into a rather scrumptious pork pie when Jake came hurtling toward them.

'Ben!' Jake puffed. 'I've been looking for you everywhere.' He stopped talking to catch his breath. 'Ricky fell on his ankle, it's swollen up like a balloon. We haven't got any substitutes so we're down to four men. Our next game is in ten minutes, can you play?'

''Course I can,' said Ben. 'But I haven't got any shorts or anything.'

'Don't worry about that we've got the spare kit that our sub was supposed to wear,'

'What happened to the sub?' asked Dan.

'Chicken pox,' replied Jake.

'Oh nice,' said Dan.

Grabbing his monkey, Ben rushed off with Jake. 'See you later,' he yelled back to his parents.

Chapter 10

With only two minutes to spare, Ben managed to change into the team's strip and get on the court.

Jake introduced him to the other team members. 'This is Bradley, and that's Simon, you've met me and Joe of course.' Jake turned to the team. 'Ben has agreed to step in at the last minute and play for us.'

'The monkey's not playing too, is he?' one of the boys asked.

Ben grinned. 'No, I'll just go and find somewhere to put him.' Looking across the court Ben could see Ricky sitting on the ground, his ankle resting on a sports bag. Beside him sat Melanie and Kate. Ben jogged over to them.

'Oh he's gorgeous! Where did you get him?' Melanie asked, smiling.

For a second Ben thought she had been referring to him but then he realised that she was talking about the monkey.

'What this thing? Oh, I won it in a basketball game. I had to score three baskets out of four.' He pretended it was no big deal.

'Oh, he's lovely. Can I hold him while you play?' asked Melanie.

'Yeah, sure.'

'Great! He'll be safe with me,' she said, stroking the soft white fur of the toy.

Ben was suddenly stuck for words and was relieved when the referee blew his whistle calling all players.

Ben scored the first basket of the match. He glanced over to Melanie to see her reaction. She leapt into the air cheering and waving the monkey up and down, like a mascot. Ben was determined to play his socks off. He was going to shine today.

The match was an important one. The winning team would go through to the final. Players scrambled after the ball, intercepted passes, and took long shots at the basket. It was a tight match but Jake's team was ahead by two points. There were just three minutes left for play when Jake called time-out.

'Okay lads, let's keep possession of the ball and defend well. Joe, you've got to stay tight on your man at all times - he's their best shooter. If they go for a basket, then make sure we get the rebound and drive the ball away as quickly as possible.'

The match was on again, everyone did exactly as Jake had ordered. Joe marked his man so closely it was a wonder he could still breathe and whenever the other team took a shot at the basket Jake jumped up and knocked the ball away.

With only twenty seconds to go, Ben blocked a pass and stole possession. If he acted quickly he could drive the ball past one defender and have a clear shot at the basket. Dodging his opponent, he took the ball underneath the net and bounced it off the backboard. Dropping onto the rim, the ball circled round and round the edge.

'Go in!' Ben willed the ball to score. Everyone held their breath, waiting to see what would happen. If the ball went in they would surely win and go through to the final. For a split second the ball stopped spinning and rested, perched above the net. 'Go in! Go in!' pleaded Ben aloud.

Obediently the ball dropped into the net and the referee blew the final whistle. Charging down the length of the court, Jake jumped onto Ben's back. He was quickly joined by Joe, Simon and Bradley. Under their weight, Ben collapsed onto the ground taking the team with him. Lying in a bedraggled heap the boys congratulated each other and marvelled at their victory.

'I can't believe you lot made it into the finals,' said a deep voice.

Ben looked up to see a tall man wearing jeans and a white T-shirt. He was probably some sort of body builder because he had muscles on his muscles. On the front of his T-shirt the words 'Powered by Christ,' were printed.

'You must be Ben,' the man said. 'Thanks for standing in for Ricky - I've just been to get an ice pack for his ankle. I'm Greg by the way.' Greg put out his hand and Ben shook it.

'Are you the coach?'

'Well, sort of, I suppose. I run the youth group at the church. We do all sorts of stuff, basketball just happens to be one of the things these guys are pretty good at.'

Ben couldn't picture someone like Greg sitting in a church listening to some stuffy old preacher droning on and on.

'Right, lads,' said Greg. 'You've got exactly one hour before the final, so go and relax for a while and meet me back here 15 minutes before the game. See you all later.' Greg ran over to a lady sitting on a bench beside the court, with her were three small children. Greg picked up the smallest one, a little girl of about two or three years of age, and twirled her round in circles. The girl screamed with delight.

'That's Greg's wife and kids,' said Jake. 'He's a great guy.'

'He looks like a "Gladiator",' said Ben.

Jake grinned. 'We're going to eat some sandwiches now, join us if you like, we've got plenty.'

'Thanks,' said Ben. 'I didn't eat much of my lunch, I'm starving now.'

Chapter 11

Last Monday's strange adventure was a million miles from Ben's thoughts today, he was having a great time. Thoughts that had plagued him for days were pushed to the back of his mind. Today he was just a normal person having a wonderful day.

Fifteen minutes before the final began, the team - along with Melanie, Kate and Ricky, gathered around Greg at the court.

'Okay, folks, we're in the final which is a lot more than we expected, so let's praise God for that. Let's ask the Lord to be with us during the match and pray for Ricky too,' said Greg.

Everyone bowed their heads and closed their eyes. Ben immediately began to feel uncomfortable. He couldn't join in with this. Suppose someone passed by and saw him. They were just making themselves look stupid.

Greg began to pray. 'Lord Jesus, we thank you for bringing Ben among us today and we thank you for the great day we're having. Lord, we pray that during this match we will show ourselves to be followers of Christ and play fairly. We pray that you will help us to accept the final outcome with a cheerful heart, whether we win or lose.'

Ben started to snigger. He didn't want to, but it all seemed so ridiculous to him that he had to fight back the giggles. This was dumb, who did Greg think he was talking to? God? Ha! Even if there was a God (and Ben was sure there wasn't) he wouldn't be a basketball fan, would he?

Greg ignored the smothered laughter and continued. 'Lord, we pray for Rick and we thank you that he was able to play in some matches today. We ask that you will help him to recover, that you will ease the pain and be with him. We ask all these things in your powerful name. Amen.'

'Amen,' said everyone except Ben.

The Hawks were the other team in the final. When they arrived on court Joe gave a long low whistle. 'This team looks hot,' he said.

Everyone watched as the Hawks warmed up by passing the ball amongst themselves and shooting baskets. They were an impressive-looking team.

'Come on, lads, there's no point in standing around admiring them,' said Greg. 'We've got a final to play!'

'Hey, Jake,' called Ben as they ran on to the court. 'What's our team called? The choir boys?'

'Actually,' replied Jake, 'we're called the Eagles.'

As soon as the game began, Ben knew the Eagles were in big trouble. The Hawks had an air-tight defence and were blocking or stealing the ball at every opportunity. They had only been playing for five minutes and already the score was 8 - 0 to the Hawks.

Seeing his team struggling, Greg called an early time-out.

'What's going on out there?' he asked when the team huddled around him. 'Yeah, they're good but so are you guys. Don't let them intimidate you. Play your game.'

'But, Greg,' said Jake, his voice filled with despair, 'we can't get near our basket, their defence is too strong.'

'Okay, okay, here's what we'll do,' said Greg. 'Let's feed the ball down to Jake or Ben and then screen them by stopping any of the defenders from getting close,' Greg turned and looked at Jake and Ben. 'It'll be down to you two to make the shots.'

'It's worth a try,' said Ben.

'Yeah,' said Jake, 'it can't get any worse.'

The game continued. Joe had possession, he passed the ball quickly to Jake. Ben and the others quickly ran over to him, screening him and blocking off the Hawks defence. Jake now had a clear shot at the basket and he wasn't going to waste this chance.

As the ball slid into the net Greg leapt into the air. 'All right! Go for it Eagles! Let's move it.'

It wasn't long before they had levelled the score. Jake scored six points and Ben scored four. The Hawks were worried. Their defence was being ripped apart and they weren't sure how they should handle it. People crowded around the court to watch the final and they liked what they were seeing. This was an exciting match and some sensational baskets were being scored. The crowd grew noisy, spurring their teams on with shouts of encouragement and advice for the players.

At just four minutes to go the Eagles were level 30 - 30. The game was now a tense display of nerve and skill. The Hawks were completely flummoxed by the Eagles' tactics and Ben could almost taste victory. Just a few more minutes, they must keep their heads and continue to

49

play to a high standard. They couldn't afford to relax, even for a moment.

Ben had the ball, he dribbled it a few yards until Jake could get free. When he passed the ball out to Jake, he ran quickly in front of him. Joe, Simon and Bradley did the same and together they formed a human wall of defence around Jake. Once again, the Hawks couldn't get anywhere near the ball. Surging up Jake took a shot at the basket. If he scored it would take them into a two-point lead which would be crucial at this stage of the game. He must score. The ball shook the rim violently and went into the net.

'Nice shot,' Ben said, turning just in time to see one of the Hawks kick Jake hard on the ankle.

Jake dropped to the ground, gripping his leg.

'What did you do that for?' Ben shouted, staring long and hard at the boy.

'Leave it, Ben, I'm okay,' said Jake. He stood up and flexed his ankle a few times. He tried to run on it but with each step he winced with pain.

The referee had seen the incident and spoke sharply to the Hawks player. 'Any more behaviour like that,' he said to the tall red-haired boy, 'and you're off the court. Do you understand me?'

The boy said nothing but sneered aggressively at Ben.

'Ignoramus,' muttered Ben back at the boy.

Just two minutes later, Joe had the ball, he looked up to pass it to Jake but Jake was double-marked. Realising this, Ben ran forwards, trying to get free and receive the pass but he came to an abrupt stop. The red-haired boy was holding on to his vest, preventing him from running. Spinning around violently Ben came face to face with the boy. 'Get off me, you idiot!'

The boy let go and Ben saw that Jake now had the ball. He rushed over to guard him. The red-haired boy ran directly into Ben's path, barging into him and sending him crashing to the ground. Ben felt as though he had collided with a brick wall. 'He did that on purpose,' thought Ben to himself, seething with rage. Furious, Ben stood up. Something hot and warm trickled along his shin. He looked down and saw a line of bright red blood oozing from a large gash on his knee. It wasn't hurting, Ben was too angry to feel pain. His rage boiled over and he automatically clenched his fists. In a fit of fury Ben stormed across the court after his enemy. If he could have breathed fire, that red-haired boy would have been a barbecued spare rib by now.

The boy had his back to Ben and didn't see him coming but then suddenly, as if sensing danger he whirled round and flinched as Ben threw a fierce heavy punch.

Chapter 12

The blow caught the red-haired boy full on the face, causing him to reel back from the force of the hit. Using a stream of swear words, Ben hurled insult after insult at the boy, who then ruthlessly set upon him. Grappling with each other they fell to the ground. Fists were flying and legs were kicking. War had broken out. The ferocious cat and dog brawl was now raging into a savage and vicious battle.

'Break it up! Break it up!' shouted the referee. He tried to separate the boys by stepping in between them but they continued fighting relentlessly.

All at once, Ben felt his arms being trapped against his sides. Greg had grabbed him from behind and was holding his arms down preventing him from punching.

'Get off me! Leave me!' Ben hollered. Some people were dragging the red-haired boy away but Ben, unable to punch, could still kick. His legs lashed out in all directions trying to reach the boy, desperate to have just one last kick. Lifting Ben off the ground, Greg physically carried him away from the fight.

'Get off me will you!' Ben shouted. 'It's got nothing to do with you.'

'Calm down, Ben,' said Greg, but Ben was still trying

to break free from Greg's hold. His face was flushed with anger and there was a cut over his left eye. Blood from the cut dripped onto his cheeks. His eye was already swelling up. When Greg felt Ben's body go limp, he knew that the fight had gone out of him. Frenzied anger had given way to exhaustion and fatigue. The fight had drained him.

'Are you all right now?' asked Greg. He released his hold on Ben. Ben stood still with his shoulders hunched. His eye was stinging, his knee throbbed and his knuckles were scraped and sore. Greg put a consoling hand on Ben's shoulder but Ben shrugged it off.

'Get lost!'

'Come on Ben, calm down now,' said Greg.

'Why should I? He deserved it - you should have let me kick his head in.' Ben glared angrily at Greg with his good eye. He didn't have any energy left but he was still mad.

The referee walked over to Greg. 'Sorry, Greg,' he said. 'Your boy's out of the game, so is the other lad. We can't have scenes like that.'

'Okay, fair enough,' said Greg. 'Sorry about that.'

The referee nodded, gave a reproachful look at Ben and then walked away.

'What are you talking about?' Ben threw his hands up in amazement and ran after the referee. 'It was his fault. He started it! He came crashing into me.'

The referee ignored Ben's outburst and blew his whistle for the game to continue.

Reluctantly, Ben sat down and watched the remainder of the game. Keeping a close eye on him, Greg decided to wait until the end of the match and then he would have a quiet word.

There were just two minutes of play left. The Eagles were down to four men but so were the Hawks. However, with Jake injured, the Eagles were at a disadvantage.

I should be playing, they need me out there. The frustration of having to sit and watch and not be able to do anything was driving him crazy. Joe, Bradley and Simon raced all over the court, doing everything they could to protect their fragile two-point lead. The Hawks had possession, they were playing like desperate men, knowing that there was very little time left. The tallest boy in the Hawks team grabbed the ball and faked his way past Bradley, sending him scurrying in the wrong direction. Taking the ball up to the net he leapt into the air with the ball raised high above his head. Almost level with the basket now, the boy gave a roar of aggression and then dunked the ball into the net. People watching the game jumped up from their seats and applauded wildly. The Hawks were elated, they had levelled the score again.

'What a basket!' shouted Greg, clapping. Ben felt sick.

'Well done, lad,' said Greg to the boy when he ran past.

'Thanks,' said the boy. 'I can't believe it, I've never slam dunked the ball before in my life.'

'Great timing,' muttered Ben angrily, 'you could have waited another week.'

At only fifteen seconds to go the Hawks scored again. Jake held his head and groaned. His leg was killing him but he knew that as the Eagles best shooter it would be down to him to save the match. Joe had possession and was driving toward the basket.

Two defenders ran up to him, putting him under pressure and Jake could see that at any second now Joe would loose the ball. Jake gritted his teeth. Ignoring his pain he ran at Joe.

'Pass it!' he screamed.

Joe passed the ball out quickly. 'Come on, Jake!' he cried.

Jake snatched the ball and ran toward the basket. Every step was sheer agony. His face contorted in pain when he took the shot and as the ball left his hands Jake stumbled. His ankle couldn't take his weight any longer and almost with relief, Jake collapsed to the ground. Craning his neck up, he looked to see if the ball would go in. He had to level the scores again, he had to save the match. The ball banged against the rim and spun away. Exhausted, Jake lowered his head on to his arms. There was no way they could win now. He had given it everything he'd got but it was all over.

The final whistle blew sending the Hawks leaping all over the court. They shrieked whoops of victory as they congratulated each other. Some of their friends ran on to the court to join in the celebrations.

Tired and dejected Simon, Bradley and Joe walked slowly over to the Hawks and shook hands with them. Then they carefully lifted Jake to his feet.

'Sorry, lads, I really tried,' said Jake.

Between them Simon and Joe carried Jake off the court.

'Here comes the true hero,' said Greg when they brought Jake to him.

Jake managed a weak smile. 'I should have made that basket, Greg.'

One of the Hawks came over to shake Jake's hand. 'Good game, I really thought you were going to get that last basket in.'

'So did I,' grinned Jake. 'Well done, you played well.'

Still sitting on the ground not far from the others, Ben could hear everything that was being said and he didn't like it at all. How could Jake say well done to those cheats. They should all be protesting to the referee by now, Greg included. Melanie had the whole team lined up and was taking photographs. 'Come on, Ben, you've got to be in the photo too,' she said.

Ben didn't want to be in their dumb photo, but he didn't want to be rude to Melanie so he got up and joined them.

'What a bunch of wounded soldiers you are,' laughed Greg looking at them.

When Melanie had finished taking pictures Ben walked away.

'Hey, Ben, hold on. I want to talk to you,' said Greg chasing after him.

'Get lost!' Ben was sick of the whole lot of them.

'Why are you so aggressive? I just want to explain something to you.'

Something in Greg's tone of voice told Ben that Greg meant to have his say. Ben stood still with his hands on his hips and looked away from Greg. His whole body language said that he wasn't in the least bit interested in anything Greg had to say, but Greg decided to say it anyway.

'I'm sorry you were provoked out there today. I know that boy was winding you up. I could see it.' Ben glanced briefly at Greg and then looked away again. 'But that doesn't excuse your behaviour today or your bad language.'

'My behaviour has got nothing to do with you,' said Ben. 'I only played for your stupid team as a favour.'

'Actually, your behaviour has everything to do with me because the Eagles are a church team and most of the boys on the team are Christians. That means that they love Jesus and when you love someone you try your best to please them. What we try to do is show that we are different, that we have something special in our lives, something that gives us peace whether we win or lose, whether we are having good times or bad. Do you understand that Ben?'

'I'll tell you one thing I do understand,' began Ben rudely, 'I understand that you lot are completely off your rockers. You're totally out of touch with reality... you're living in cloud cuckoo land.'

Greg shook his head sadly. 'Before I knew about Jesus my life was probably a lot like yours. All I cared about was me and my rights, but when I found out about Jesus he changed all that and he can change you too.'

'Change me into what?' Ben scoffed. 'A Dalek?'

Greg ignored Ben's sarcasm and carried on speaking. 'Look, Ben, my life is brand new. When I'm happy - I praise Jesus. When I'm sad - I tell him about it. He's always there for me.'

Ben listened quietly to Greg and when he had finished speaking he laughed. The laugh was full of bitterness and scorn. 'You lot need to get a life,' he said.

'Oh, we've got life all right,' said Greg. 'God loved us so much that He sent Jesus, His only Son, to this world to die for us and now we'll never ever have to die but will live forever. It tells us that in the Bible - John chapter 3, verse 16.'

'You're crazy. Everyone dies in the end,' said Ben. He wanted to see Greg wriggle out of that one.

'You're right, Ben, but when I die, I know that I will go to be with God. I'll carry on living in Heaven and I'll be able to see my friend Jesus, face to face. What's going to happen to you when you die?'

Ben sneered while he tried to think up a good enough answer. 'They'll bury me in a wooden box and the worms will get me,' he said defiantly.

'Well, Ben, that's definitely something for you to look forward to.' Greg smiled. 'I think I prefer my version, don't you?'

'I'm going to meet my Mum and Dad,' Ben huffed. He was about to walk away when Jake called out to him.

'Hey, Ben, thanks for playing for us today. Why don't you come to church tomorrow? We've got an American man coming to talk to us. He used to play for a professional team but now he's a missionary. It should be really interesting.'

This was the last straw.

'I wouldn't come to your stupid church if you paid me. You lot are a bunch of brainless wimps. Church is for morons.' Ben shouted angrily.

'Does that mean you're not coming then?' Jake asked.

Everyone erupted into loud laughter which made Ben even more annoyed. He searched for something piercing to say, but when he could find nothing he simply threw them a look of contempt, turned on his heel and marched away. They were the biggest group of losers he had ever met.

'Benjamin! What's happened to you?'

Ben's parents were mortified when they saw the condition that their son was in. 'Was it a basketball match you were in or bare knuckle fight?' asked his father.

Ben shrugged. Taking out a white embroidered handkerchief his mother began dabbing at the blood on Ben's face.

'Stop it, Mum! Just leave me alone will you.'

'Now hold on a minute!' said his father. 'I don't know what you've been involved in today, but you certainly do not take it out on your mother.'

'It's all right, Dan, he's upset.'

'I don't care if he is! That does not excuse him for talking to you in that way.'

No one spoke during the long journey back to the cottage. Ben sulked in that back seat of the car. He knew one thing for sure, tomorrow he would go to the beach and look for the stone.

Chapter 13

It was 5 am when Ben woke up the next morning. He looked in the mirror to see how his eye was getting on. The swelling had gone down but the whole eye was heavily bruised. Ben grinned at his reflection. He had a black eye. What a pity his friends back home wouldn't see it.

Ben dressed himself quickly and then quietly crept downstairs. Opening the fridge door he looked to see what he could take for his lunch. There was plenty of ham and cheese but Ben couldn't be bothered to make himself a sandwich. He took a pork pie and a piece of quiche, and grabbed a can of Coke. That would have to do. Packing his meagre lunch into his rucksack, Ben set off for the beach.

Outside, the morning air was refreshing, the grass all around was damp with dew. His trainers squelched with each step he took. Ben breathed deeply. The scent of the distant sea was in the air making it smell clean and healthy, it was already giving Ben an appetite. He quickened his pace a little. Suppose the stone had been washed away in the tide or what if someone else had found it and taken it away...

Running on to the beach Ben's eyes anxiously scanned

over the pebbles. Last night's deposits of shells and dead crabs were lying amongst the stones but nothing out of the ordinary could be seen. Having missed his breakfast, Ben decided to eat his lunch. Scrambling on to a large rock, he sat down to eat. It was probably the same rock Ben had sat on last time he came to the beach, but he couldn't be sure. Even while he ate, his eyes skimmed across the stones, searching for the extraordinary one he had found before.

Opening his can, Ben wondered what Jake and the others were doing but then he remembered that it was Sunday and they would all be at church. He suddenly realised that he had left his monkey with Melanie. That would mean that either Jake or Greg would have an excuse to come and visit him, he didn't think Melanie would bring it back.

Aggravated by this, Ben tossed his empty can as far as he could throw it. It fell on to the pebbles, just yards away from the sea. Taking up a handful of stones, he began to aim them one by one at the can. Most of his throws missed, but one hit with a resounding ping. The can bounced up into the air and fell on to some sand, directly in front of the sea. A wave swept in and carried the can away. Ben carried on tossing stones at it but it was even harder now that it was a moving target. He was about to lob another stone when he froze. It was an icy cold morning but Benjamin could feel beads of hot perspiration trickling down his back. In just the spot where the tin can had been, a stone was sending out quick flashes of silver light, it had to be the one.

Crouching down low, Benjamin was almost too scared to touch the stone but too excited not to seize the challenge. Reaching out tentatively he touched it ever so gently, just with the tip of his finger. As it had before, the stone immediately stopped flashing. It lay there looking like any other ordinary stone on the beach, only Ben knew it was not. It sat their waiting for him, daring him to pick it up, laughing at him even. Ben hesitated. He wanted to experience another terrifying journey into the unknown but he wasn't sure whether or not he was ready for another white knuckle trip.

Gulls circled overheard, their piercing cries seemed to say, 'Do it, do it.'

Ben swallowed. What if he couldn't get back? What if he got stuck out their forever? Maybe he should give this a little more thought.

'Do it, do it,' screeched the sea gulls.

Stretching out his hand, Ben's fingers lingered over the stone. Taking a deep breath of courage he closed his eyes tightly and grasped the mysterious orb. Even though he could not see, Ben knew that the sky had gone black. The sea and the wind joined forces to create a terrorising rush of energy. Ben wanted to run. He had changed his mind, this wasn't a good idea after all. His rucksack swept up into the air and slapped Ben's face before being blown away by the power of the wind. Not knowing what had hit him, Ben gave a shout of fear. He opened his eyes to pitch black darkness. At once, the wind stopped howling and the sea was still. The sky suddenly became white. Ben had to shield his eye against the brightness. His body tensed when he felt himself rising from the ground and being sucked helplessly into air.

*   *   *   *   *

Ben looked up to see a pretty young girl of about eight or nine years of age. He seemed to be in some sort of town.

There were lots of barefoot children running around on dusty roads.

The young girl suddenly screamed and ran behind Ben. A boy with jet black hair and a dirty face advanced toward her, looking menacing. The girl shrieked with laughter. Pulling Ben first one way and then the other the girl used him as a shield to protect her from the boy. More children raced around the corner but when they saw the boy they stopped in their tracks and ran in the opposite direction. Seizing his chance the boy chased after them and yelling, 'LEPER,' he touched one of the running children on the back. When they had gone Ben turned to look at the girl.

'What's going on? What does 'leper' mean?'

'That is two questions and thou hast not even answered my one question yet,' she said.

'Sorry,' said Ben. 'What was your question?'

The girl sighed. 'I asked thee, who art thou?'

'Oh, yeah, I'm Ben,' he replied.

'Benjamin! How beautiful is thy name.'

'Yeah? Well what's your name then?' Ben asked.

'I am Rachel and that is my house.' She pointed to a small flat building. 'What happened to thy eye?'

'Oh, er... I had a fight,' answered Ben.

'Thou art very brave,' said Rachel. She smiled at Ben. 'Hast thou cometh here to see the teacher?'

'Come here to see a teacher? No fear! I'm on my six-weeks holiday,' said Ben.

Rachel looked puzzled. She decided that Benjamin was truly an odd person but she liked him. Studying him carefully, Rachel walked around him, seeing him from different angles. Benjamin began to feel rather uncomfortable.

'So what does 'leper' mean?' he asked.

'It is a game we play. One of us pretends to be the leper and chaseth after everyone. If the leper touches thee then thou art a leper too.'

'Oh, we call that game "it".' If you get touched then you're "it",' Benjamin explained.

'Yes but what is "it"?' Rachel asked.

'Well, I don't know really. What is 'leper'?'

'Thou knoweth not?' Rachel seemed surprised. 'A leper is he that hath leprosy.'

'I think I've heard of that,' said Ben. 'What exactly is it?'

'It is the death,' Rachel answered in hushed tones. 'O wretched disease that it is. It killeth man, woman or child. It drains the life from thee until thou canst hardly walk. It can taketh away thy sight. Father saw a leper once and his face had been eaten away by leprosy.' Rachel wrinkled her nose in disgust and shivered. Just then a lady came out of Rachel's house and shouted.

'Rachel, thy food is ready.'

'What is thy father's name?' Rachel asked Benjamin.

'What? Why? It's erm... it's Dan,' he answered. Rachel sure was a strange one.

'Wait here, Benjamin, I shall return,' said Rachel. She ran into her house. After a minute or so Rachel came out again and ran over to Ben.

'That was a quick meal,' joked Benjamin. Rachel laughed loudly.

'Come to my house, Benjamin, my father is waiting to greet thee. My mother hath prepared fresh bread.' Clasping Ben's hand Rachel led him into her home.

'Father, this is Benjamin, son of Daniel,' said Rachel pushing Ben toward her father.

'A fine boy,' said Rachel's father.

64

He was an enormous man with a thick curly brown beard.

'This is my mother,' said Rachel to Ben. 'Mother, this is Benjamin, son of Daniel.'

Rachel's mother smiled shyly at Ben.

'Hello,' said Benjamin. 'Pleased to meet you.'

'Sit with us, Benjamin. Eat, we have plenty,' said Rachel's father.

The smell of home baking wafted up to Ben's nostrils. He was starving after his sparse lunch. Meat and bread were served at the table. The bread was still warm and melted in Ben's mouth. It tasted delicious. Benjamin ate very well despite the fact that Rachel was beaming at him the whole time.

'Where is thy family, Benjamin?' asked Rachel's father.

'Erm, not far away. In a village,' Ben answered. He hoped that this information would be enough.

Rachel's mother poured some wine for them all. Ben was surprised to see Rachel drinking it too.

'And now, Benjamin, son of Daniel, I understand thou seeketh to marry our daughter,' said Rachel's father.

Spitting out his wine, Benjamin choked. 'I seek to do what?'

'Father is looking for a husband for me and thou hast won my heart,' Rachel explained.

'But... but you're only... I'm only fourteen!' spluttered Benjamin.

'My friend Hannah is only eight and her marriage is arranged already. She is betrothed to marry on her fifteenth birthday,' said Rachel.

'But I... I can't marry you. I can't marry anybody - not yet anyway.'

Rachel looked disappointed.

'I must meet with thy father. I shall speak with him. It is better that way,' said Rachel's father to Ben.

'Yes, Rachel,' said her mother, 'cease thy searching for a husband and leave it to thy father.'

'But mother, my heart longs for Benjamin, son of Daniel.'

Ben swallowed hard.

The door of the house burst open and a tall thin man leaned in.

'He is here! The teacher is here. Come quickly,' he called.

Rachel gave a squeal of delight as her parents left their food and ran from the house.

'Come, Benjamin, let us go.' Grabbing Ben's hand, Rachel pulled him up and led him out of the house. Outside people were rushing along the streets, the air filled with their excited babble. As they followed the people, Ben noticed that once again he was wearing a dress of some description and the same pair of sandals that he had worn before. This time he didn't mind quite so much as he had come to realise that these clothes were all the rage here.

Chapter 14

The teacher was a man in his early thirties. He didn't seem to mind that everyone was crowding around him, all talking at once, everyone wanting to tell him something or ask him a question. He smiled at people, touched them, laughed with them. He really loved them.

'Leper!'

A child's voice rang out from the crowd. Everyone ignored it, they were far too happy to be with the teacher to worry about some silly children's game.

'Leper!'

The cry went up again only this time louder and with more urgency. It was the same boy that Rachel had been playing leper with earlier.

'Reuben, son of Amos, be still!'

That was probably Rachel's way of telling him to shut up, Ben thought to himself.

The boy's mouth fell open. His eyes were filled with horror. He was pointing to something behind Rachel and Ben. Together they turned around and saw a man, in torn rags, stumbling toward them. His head was covered by filthy cloths that he held up to conceal his face.

'LEPER!.. LEPER!.. LEPER!' screamed Rachel. 'Run Benjamin!'

Mass panic broke out in the crowd. People were running back to their houses at speeds that would have made the current Olympic 100 metres champion jealous. Rachel was gone. The children were gone. The crowd was gone. Only Benjamin remained. He wanted to run but his feet wouldn't move. The leper was coming closer to him.

'Please don't touch me,' said Ben. His voice was trembling. There were swellings and bumps all over the man's face. His hands were gnarled and twisted. His feet were wrapped in blood-stained bandages. The leper didn't even glance at Ben as he limped forwards. He had come to see the teacher and his eyes never left him once.

The teacher stood still. He hadn't run away like the others and he didn't seem afraid at all. The leper approached the teacher and Ben was sure that at any second the teacher would tell him to stop and stay where he was but he didn't. He allowed the leper to get closer and closer until they were almost touching each other. The teacher's eyes looked directly at the man as he uncovered his face. When Ben saw how horrible the man's face was he had to close his eyes and look away with revulsion, but the teacher didn't even flinch. The leper fell to his knees in front of him.

'Sir,' he said with tears flowing down his face, 'if thou wilt, thou canst make me clean.'

The teacher looked at the man but said nothing and the man said it again.

'Thou canst make me clean... if thou wilt.' He had waited, planned, dreamed about this moment for so long, and now the emotion, mixed with relief at having finally spoken to the teacher was all too much for him. He wept loudly until the teacher touched him on the shoulder. The leper let out a gasp of shock. He couldn't remember the last time someone had touched him.

The teacher smiled. 'I will,' he said simply, 'be clean.' He placed his hands on the leper's face. He was actually touching his open sores! Ben winced. Rachel would be so upset now that the teacher had caught leprosy...

The leper was weeping on to the teacher's hands and he was shaking. 'Thou wilt make me clean?' he asked, smiling through his tears. He could hardly believe it.

Ben's eyes widened when he saw fresh, clear, smooth skin was appearing all over the man's face. The leper touched his face in amazement. He looked at his hands, pulled his sleeves up to look at his arms and then he began laughing. The man jumped up and down and started dancing and all the time he kept saying, 'Thank you, my Lord, thank you!' He was completely normal now, there wasn't a blemish on him. His face was a glowing picture of health.

Ben felt a shiver of excitement rush up and down his spine. What had he seen here today and how did the teacher do that? Ben watched as the man who had once been riddled with leprosy sat down and began to unwind the bandages from his feet. His feet were perfect. There was no blood or sores to be seen. How could this be?

'I am clean! I am clean! The teacher maketh me clean!' The man could hardly speak, he was so overcome with joy.

'Benjamin, son of Daniel, where art thou my beloved?' sang Rachel's voice but she was too late.

Ben was suddenly engulfed in a kaleidoscope of colours. They whirled faster and faster until he was dizzy and disorientated. He floated into a calm sea of darkness and then all was still.

When Benjamin awoke he was once again lying on the doorstep of the cottage, his rucksack by his side.

'Quick! Get up,' he said to himself. 'I can't let Dad see me sleeping on the doorstep again.' He banged on the door of the cottage and his mother answered.

'Benjamin, where have you been? We were worried sick.'

'Sorry,' said Ben. 'I went to the beach.'

'Well, come in now, we've got a visitor. Rachel's here.'

'What!' Benjamin took three steps backwards in shock. How could Rachel be here?

'Yes, Rachel, she's the lady we nearly ran over last week,' his mother said. 'Isn't it a lovely name. I was just telling her that if you'd have been born a girl I would have named you Rachel.'

Ben shuddered.

'Don't you like that name?' she asked him.

Ben thought aloud for a moment. 'Rachel, daughter of Claire? No, I prefer Benjamin, son of Daniel,' he said as he walked inside. His mother raised her eyebrows but said nothing.

Chapter 15

For three days Benjamin longed to return to the beach but
his parents had made plans for the family to do a spot of
sightseeing. Rachel (the old lady) had loaned them a book
which listed all the 'interesting' places to visit within a
25-mile radius. Benjamin saw enough pottery workshops,
country mansions and farms to last him a lifetime.

'Will it be all right if I go to the beach tomorrow?' he
asked his parents, hoping that they had not already made
plans.

'Of course you can,' said his mother. 'I need to get
down to some serious writing anyway, I've been far too
lazy these last few days.'

'I'll come to the beach with you,' said his father.
Benjamin looked uneasy.

'What's the matter with you? Don't you want your
old man hanging around with you? Frightened I'll cramp
your style?'

'No,' said Benjamin defensively. 'I'd just planned to
go on my own, that's all.'

Claire suddenly looked up. 'Oh, I see,' she said.

Benjamin and Dan both looked confused.

'What?' Dan asked.

'Oh nothing. Dan, don't forget you promised you would let me read my work aloud to you so you can give me some constructive criticism and a bit of feedback,' she said.

'Did I?' Dan asked. It was the first he'd heard of it.

'Yes, you did, darling,' Claire said. She nodded at her husband, and said each word slowly, encouraging him to agree. 'So you can't go with Ben, can you?' Now she was shaking her head. 'No, you can't.'

Dan was completely baffled by this conversation, so was Ben.

'Sorry, Ben, looks like I can't go with you after all,' he conceded.

When Ben had gone to bed later that night, Dan turned to his wife, 'What was all that nonsense about earlier? I didn't have a clue what you were going on about. Do you know something I don't know?'

'A mother knows these things,' Claire smiled. She was looking like a cat that had just caught the canary.

'Claire! Will you stop being so cryptic and tell me in plain English what it is you think you know.'

'It's obvious,' she beamed. 'Ben must have a girlfriend. I bet it's that girl he was talking to at the festival... the one we saw carrying the orangutang that Benjamin won - and that's another thing, where is the monkey now?'

'I don't know,' said Dan. 'Where is it?'

'Dan, you're so slow!' said his wife. 'Can't you work it out? Ben must have given it to that girl. I think that's so sweet.' Claire sighed and smiled at her husband.

Laughing quietly, Dan said, 'You're terrible! Are all women like this or is it just you?

'I'll tell you another thing, Dan,' she added, ignoring

her husband's comments, 'I bet Ben got his black eye because he was fighting over her with another boy.'

'Or from fighting with her,' Dan joked

'Oh Dan, that's typical of you,' said Claire, 'where's your sense of romance?'

'You can't say Ben's got a girlfriend. You don't know that for sure.'

Claire tapped the side of her nose with her finger.

'Call it women's intuition.'

*   *   *   *   *

Ben spent three hours on the beach the next morning. Raking over the pebbles with his fingers and crawling along the beach on his hands and knees. He searched relentlessly. Several times he rushed across the beach thinking he could see flashes of light only to discover a piece of silver chewing gum wrapper glinting in the sun. It was so ironic. Now that he wanted the stone, wanted the adventure, now that he wasn't scared any more, it was nowhere to be found. Dejected, Ben walked back to the cottage, his shoulders drooping with disappointment and his heart heavy.

'You're back early, you usually stay all day when you go to the beach,' his mother said when Ben returned home.

'I got fed up,' he told her flatly.

'Want something to eat?'

'No thanks, I'm just going to lie down in my room for a while. I've got a bit of a headache.'

A five-minute conversation followed during which Ben's mother asked him if he wanted an aspirin or a paracetamol, did he have a temperature and was the pain over one eye or did it spread over his whole forehead?

When Benjamin eventually closed the door of his room, he was thankful for the peace and quiet. Being miserable always made him feel tired and right now all he wanted to do was sleep.

It must have been an hour later when Jake knocked on the cottage door. His ankle was in plaster and he had a crutch tucked under each arm. At his feet sat Ben's monkey. Dan opened the door.

'Hello, I'm Jake. Is Ben in please?'

'Yes, he is, come in.' Dan picked up the monkey and opened the door wide so that Jake could manoeuvre himself through the doorway. 'Ben! Visitor,' he yelled up the stairs.

'Goodness me, you didn't walk all the way here like that did you?' Claire asked when Jake entered the living room. She pointed to a chair. 'Sit down, Ben won't be long.'

'Thanks,' said Jake. ' My Dad dropped me here in his car, he's coming back for me in twenty minutes.'

'What happened to your leg?' Dan asked.

'I had an accident while playing basketball. I ran on it while it was injured and that made it worse... they say it's a slight fracture, it's not as bad as it looks though.'

'Have you got any brothers or sisters Jake?' asked Claire.

'Yes, I've got a twin sister, Melanie. You probably saw her at the festival,' replied Jake.

'I don't know where Ben is,' said Dan swiftly changing the subject. 'I'll call him again.'

'No need,' said Ben moodily, as he walked into the room. 'I'm here.'

'Right, well I'll start making lunch. Dan, you can give me a hand,' said Claire. She got up and flashed her eyes at her husband. Dan followed her out.

'You forgot your orangutang,' said Jake. 'I brought it back for you.'

'Thanks,' said Ben.

'Nice eye.' Jake grinned but Ben remained blank faced. He had hoped to break the ice with a bit of friendly conversation but he could tell that Ben wasn't going to make this easy.

'Look, Ben, things got a bit hot under the collar at the basketball match but that doesn't mean we can't still be friends. We'd still like you to come down to the village and play ball with us - if you want to that is.'

Ben groaned. 'No way, not when you guys keep droning on about church and Jesus and all that stuff. I'm not religious. No one in my family is.'

'Yeah, well, neither am I,' said Jake.

'What? You could have fooled me,' Ben jeered.

'It's true, Ben. I'm not into religion and rules, special prayers that you have to learn or wearing funny robes... I've got a real relationship with Jesus. That might seem hard to understand but he's my friend and I talk to him just like I'm talking to you now. Jesus has made such a big difference to my life and I love him.'

'How can you love someone you can't even see?' Ben asked.

'Well, I'll admit it's not always easy, but the Bible tells me all about him and what he did for me and the more I learn, the more I love him,' said Jake. 'Jesus was a powerful, exciting man when he was on earth - and he still is now.'

'Sorry,' said Ben with a sarcastic laugh, 'but I don't think the Bible has got anything exciting to say at all.'

'Have you even read a page of it?' Jake asked. Ben

didn't reply. 'Exciting? The Bible is mind blowing! Jesus healed blind people, he made deaf people hear, he cured lepers and demon-possessed people.'

'Hold on. Hold on,' said Ben. 'How do you know about leprosy?'

'Like I said,' replied Jake, 'It's in the Bible. Jesus healed lots of people who had leprosy.'

'Do you know how disgusting leprosy is?' Ben asked his mind suddenly flashing back to the scene he had witnessed a few days ago.

'Well, I know it could make a man go blind, and that lepers had to live in caves away from everyone else,' replied Jake.

'That's nothing. It could cover a man from head to toe in sores and swellings. His whole face could be like a balloon of enormous decaying bumps. His fingers and toes could be eaten away by the disease and he...'

'All right Ben! Stop! I've got to have my lunch when I get in.' Jake smiled at Ben who suddenly burst out laughing.

'Sorry,' he said.

'That's okay. So what are you, some sort of leprosy expert?' Teased Jake.

'You could say that,' replied Ben. 'Does it really say that Jesus healed lepers in the Bible?'

'Sure it does. Want me to read a bit about leprosy to you?' Jake took a small New Testament from his back pocket and flicked through the pages. 'Here we are. Luke, chapter 5 . "While Jesus was in one of the towns, a man came along who was covered in leprosy. When he saw Jesus he fell with his face to the ground and begged him, 'If you want to, you can make me clean.' Jesus reached out his hand and touched the man, 'I do want to,' he said, 'be clean,' and immediately the leprosy left him.'"

Ben sat quietly listening. It was just like he had seen. The hairs on his arms stood up and he could feel a tingling sensation creeping up his spine.

'What does it say happened next?' Ben asked.

'Oh, well, Jesus tells the man not to tell anyone because he knew that if they knew, then crowds and crowds of people would all want to see him doing his miracles. Jesus didn't want to be some glamorous superstar, famous for his healings. That wasn't the reason that he came. He wanted people to see him as a Saviour.'

Ben wasn't sure what a Saviour really was but he knew that there was no way the leper he had seen could keep quiet about his healing. 'I bet that man didn't keep it to himself. I bet he was so happy he told everyone.'

'Yeah, he did actually and people from all over the place started bringing their sick relatives to Jesus for healing. Eventually it got so bad that Jesus had to go into hiding so that he could pray quietly on his own.'

'Do you think anyone ever called him "Teacher"?' Ben asked.

'Absolutely,' replied Jake. 'Jesus is often referred to as 'teacher' in other parts of the Bible... I thought you didn't know anything about Jesus?' Jake was surprised but Ben didn't say where he had come by all this knowledge.

Could the teacher be Jesus? Outside a car horn sounded.

'Jake, I think that's your father,' Ben's mother called.

Carefully, Jake stood up. 'I'm glad we had this talk Ben, I've never met a leprosy expert before.'

'Thanks for bringing the monkey back,' said Ben smiling.

When Jake had gone, Ben rushed upstairs, grabbed his jacket and rushed downstairs again. All this was done with the maximum amount of noise and clatter.

'What's going on?' his father asked, looking bemused

'Can't stop for lunch - I'm going down to the beach. See you later.' Ben looked at his mother and decided to kiss her.

BANG went the cottage door as he left.

'What on earth was all that about?' Dan said looking at the space where just a few seconds ago his son had stood.

Claire smiled secretly. 'It's obvious. Ben fell out with Melanie this morning and he came home broken-hearted. She probably went home in tears and sent her brother Jake here to try and patch things up. Bringing the monkey back was just a good excuse to come over. Well, Jake's told Ben that Melanie is sorry and now Ben's dashing out to see her. He looked so happy didn't he?'

'Is this all women's intuition?' Dan asked.

'You'd better believe it is,' said Claire proudly.

Chapter 16

He had to find the stone. He had to find out for sure if the teacher really was the same Jesus that Jake had read about in the Bible. Somehow Ben had never imagined Jesus to be a man, just a baby. All those school plays in infant school about Mary and Joseph and baby Jesus. Once when he was six he was chosen to play the part of Joseph. It was a proud day. Ben wore his mother's best white tea towel on his head, secured with a piece of black ribbon. Dan always loved to tell the story of how Benjamin had been so caught up with the applause of the audience that he refused to leave the stage, even when all the other children had gone.

He stood there beaming at all the mums and dads and then encouraged by their laughter, little Joseph started dancing, or at least trying to. In the end he was carried off the stage by Mr Thomlinson, the Headteacher. Ben still blushed at the memory of that day. Hold on! That first adventure the one with the missing boy. Could that have been Jesus as he was growing up? What was it the boy said? 'Didn't you know I'd be in my Father's house,' or words to that effect anyway. But he wasn't in his

Father's house, was he? His mother and father were searching everywhere for him. He was in the temple, and that was some sort of church wasn't it, and don't people say that the church is meant to be the house of God. Was he Jesus? Was he saying that God was his Father? Ben had to go back. He simply must.

As he ran on to the beach, his heart was suddenly gripped by the fear that again, he might be unsuccessful. This morning he had spent hours searching for the stone, suppose he never found it again.

Ben sat on 'his' rock, looking out at the sparkling sea. It was a warm afternoon. A gentle breeze ruffled his hair. Above him the gulls were gliding lazily in circles.

Shielding his eyes from the radiance of the sun, Ben looked up at them. He wasn't going to comb the beach looking for the stone. No, the stone had always found him. He would wait patiently, soon it would reveal itself.

After an hour of sitting, nagging doubts crept up on Ben. Maybe he should make the effort to look. Jumping off of the rock he stretched his long limbs and then smiled. Stepping aside, Ben could see the stone. It had been there all the time.

'So that's where you're hiding,' said Ben, and then realising he was talking to a stone he laughed. 'Get real, Ben!'

Without an ounce of fear, Benjamin grabbed the stone, his fingers firmly curled around it. His feet left the ground and he was hauled violently into the air. The wind yanked him aggressively into the spinning colours and once again he was tumbling into the chaos of a vibrant psychedelic sky. He began to feel delirious. When would it end? The swirling increased in speed until Ben thought he would go crazy. It had to stop. Please let it stop!

Roars of loud laughter filled the air. Ben could hear some men's deep, rough voices raised in boisterous conversation. In the background, Ben was sure he could hear the gentle lapping of waves. Was he still on the beach? He couldn't be sure where he was. There seemed to be a large blanket covering his head and Ben fought furiously to get out from under it.

Mercifully he found a corner of the blanket and peeped out. He groaned quietly when he saw that he was surrounded by a group of big, strong men. None of them seemed to be aware that he was there but Ben still felt afraid. What am I doing here? I'm some sort of stowaway on a boat filled with gruesome burly men who are going to toss me overboard the very second they discover me.

'This doesn't look good,' Ben thought to himself. 'How am I going to get out of here?'

As he peered out into the moonlight, he suddenly realised that he had seen these men before. They had been with the teacher when he arrived at Rachel's town.

They weren't vicious men. They were the teacher's friends. They were the one's who tried to calm the crowd down when the leper first appeared. Ben breathed a sigh of sheer relief. There was no way these men would throw him overboard.

'The wind is rising - we must row,' went up a cry from one of the men. 'A storm is coming.'

Ben peeked out again to see the men rushing to the oars and beginning to row.

He had always wanted to row a real boat, not just one of those kid's ones that you find on park lakes. He watched, aware that the boat was now moving through the water. With a sinking feeling Ben remembered that he was not a very good sailor. He had been sea-sick on the ferry from Dover to Calais last year when the school went on a day-trip to France. It was dark and the waves were growing stronger. The men struggled to gain control over their boat as it was buffeted by the waves.

'Do not fear, we have been in many storms such as this,' cried one of the men above the wind.

Benjamin was semi-relieved. At least they knew what they were doing... or thought they did. Gathering more gusto the waves crashed against the sides of the boat, rocking it heavily. The gales were blowing stronger now, a shroud of sea-mist appeared and the sea took on a desolate, eerie quality. Benjamin began to tremble. This was like one of those horror movies he had seen where any second now something hideous would jump out at you.

Feeling even more sick, Benjamin wished desperately that he could get some fresh air. The blanket he was under reeked of fish. As he raised his head slightly, he was sure he saw something. He squinted his eyes, no, his imagination was running away with him... but there was definitely something over there on the water.

'Row, men! We must reach the land,' shouted someone. Vigorously they rowed for their lives but it was impossible to steer the ship against such a fierce wind. Drips of perspiration were falling into the mens' eyes as they fought against the storm.

Suddenly, through the mist, Ben saw the shadowy form of a man walking across the sea.

One of the men in the boat stood up and stared across the dark waters.

'Sit down and row Peter!' Someone shouted, but the man that they called Peter stood trembling.

'G... G... Gho... Ghost!' Peter screamed.

The other men dropped their oars and ran to the side of the boat to see. Hysteria broke out and the men, filled with fear began crying out into the dark storm.

'Leave us be!' yelled one man. Ben had never been so afraid in his life. Nothing could have prepared him for this sight.

A voice from out of the wind suddenly called out, 'Do not panic. It is I, do not be afraid.'

A deathly silence fell over the men and then one of them said, 'Is it our Master?'

'That cannot be the teacher,' said another.

Ben was shivering now and not just from the cold.

'Lord, if it really is you,' said Peter, 'then tell me to walk to you over the water.'

'What? You can't do that,' muttered Ben 'you'll drown... don't be crazy Peter, it might be a trap.' Nobody heard Ben, their eyes were glued to the figure hovering on the water.

'Come,' the silhouette beckoned for Peter to step out on to the sea. Peter climbed out of the boat. He looked straight at the figure as he bravely put one foot and then the other on to the water. Fearlessly, he began to walk over the waves. His feet never once went beneath their surface. Ben couldn't believe what he was seeing, was this some sort of illusion, some sort of trick... but how?

Peter's eyes were determined, he just had to hold his nerve for a few steps more; but when he was only six or seven strides away a strong gust of wind blustered around him, whipping the waves up around his legs. Peter looked anxiously back at the boat.

'Keep going Peter,' the men shouted.

Scared, Peter began concentrating hard. He looked at his feet, willing them not to sink. With every step he plunged deeper and deeper into the sea. Peter stretched out his hand and screamed in a voice rasping with fright, 'Lord, save me!'

'Peter!' shouted the men as they watched, powerless to do anything to save their friend. The teacher immediately grabbed Peter's hand and pulled him out of the sea, until he was once again standing on the surface of the water

'Oh, man of little faith,' said the teacher, 'why didst thou doubt?

He got so far, why did he lose his nerve? Ben could almost feel the teacher's disappointment.

Peter looked ashamed as he and the teacher, walking on the water, made their way back to the boat. When they reached the side of the ship, the wind stopped howling and the sea was calm.

No one could speak, everyone was too stunned by the display of power that they had just witnessed. How could anyone walk over water? Benjamin wasn't sure why but he was suddenly so overcome with emotion that tears flowed easily from his eyes.

'Truly thou art the Son of God,' said one of the men bowing at the teacher's feet.

With appalling timing, Ben realised that he was about to be sick. Struggling to get out from underneath the blanket, he suddenly felt dizzy. Looking up he saw the sky bathed in a mass of whirling colour and began to panic. 'Oh no, I don't want to go home yet. I've got to talk to the teacher,' he cried, but he was powerless to alter anything. Sucked up out of the boat, Ben found himself caught up in the wild tornado of the sky.

Chapter 17

The spinning finally stopped. With enormous relief Benjamin relaxed. Thoughts and visions flitted silently through his mind and like a summer breeze they were soothing, adding to the tranquillity of the moment. Ben dreamed of Zach, Rachel and Peter. He saw the man who had been cured of leprosy and imagined that he too had been able to walk on the water. In his dream he sat on the boat beside the teacher and talked to him about all his adventures so far. He finally got to ask the question that had puzzled him for so long. He asked the teacher if he really was the same person that Jake talked about in the Bible. 'Are you Jesus?' Ben asked.

The teacher looked at him carefully, smiled and said -

*   *   *   *   *

'What's that racket?'

Ben sat up abruptly. Where was he? What on earth was going on here? He was sitting in someone's house which was packed with people and full of the most terrible noise Ben had ever heard. Wailing and crying at the tops of their voices, people staggered around the house. A man sitting beside Ben banged heavily on some kind of gong and shouted cries of despair each time he struck it. Monotonous notes from a wooden pipe that was being played like a flute incited the people to even louder shrieks of misery. It was a horrendous din. What on earth were they so heartbroken about? Maybe it was a funeral. Ben could see a woman sitting in the middle of the room. She seemed to be crying harder than the others and had several people surrounding her. This was dreadful. Ben had to get out. Making his way out of the house Ben wondered what he was doing here. Surely he should have been waking up on the cottage doorstep by now. Did this mean that he would never get back?

A boy of about 15 or 16 years of age was sitting on the ground outside. In his hands he held a stick and with it he angrily scratched letters on to the dusty road.

'Hi,' said Ben.

'What is high?' the boy asked.

'Sorry, no, I didn't mean high as in how high is that mountain, I just meant hi, as in hello.'

'But hello is only a greeting, how canst it be high?'

'Oh forget it,' said Benjamin losing patience, 'it's no big deal.'

'What is a 'big deal'?'

'Oh brother!' sighed Benjamin. 'And yes, I know you're not my brother.'

The boy looked at Benjamin sympathetically. 'Thy grief hast made thou speak nonsense. Thou speaketh like a foolish man.'

'Yeah? Well you wanna listen to yourself sometime,' Ben said sarcastically, 'thou soundeth like a moron.'

Pleased with himself, Ben folded his arms in front of his chest and sat down beside the boy. Shuffling to one side, the boy put a greater distance between himself and Ben.

'I'm Benjamin,' said Ben. 'What's your name?'

'Simeon,' replied the boy gruffly.

'What's going on in there?' Ben asked. 'It sounds dreadful in that house.'

'They are mourning,' said Simeon. 'Lazarus was a very good man.'

'How did he die?'

'The same way everyone does, he got sick,' said Simeon.

'Was he really old?'

'Lazarus? Old?' Simeon laughed bitterly. 'Lazarus was a young man - not yet married.' He sighed heavily, 'I will miss him.'

Ben sat quietly out of respect for Simeon's feelings, but then Simeon grew angry.

'I blame the teacher!'

'The teacher?' Now Ben was really curious. 'What's the teacher got to do with all this?'

Throwing down his stick, Simeon said, 'The teacher is meant to be a good friend of Lazarus. All day long Lazarus would tell me about him, saying that he is the Son of God and that exciting things are to come, but now look,' Simeon sneered, 'Lazarus lies cold in his grave and the teacher cannot be found.'

'Maybe the teacher didn't know his friend was ill,' Ben suggested. It seemed hard to believe that the teacher couldn't be bothered to come to his friend's funeral.

'He knew!' spat Simeon. 'Lazarus' sisters sent word to him several days ago saying, "Lord the one thou loveth is sick", but he did not come. He never even came for the burial.'

'Perhaps he never got the message, Simeon.'

Simeon's face became enraged. 'Why dost thou maketh excuses for the teacher? I say teacher but he is nothing more than a carpenter from Nazareth. He cannot really heal people as they say and that is why he didst not come! He knoweth he hath no real power and so he stayeth away.' Simeon was silent for a second. 'I've never actually seen him heal anyone, it is all talk. When he was asked to come here and heal before our very eyes, he did not come.

'But Simeon, didn't he heal lepers?' Benjamin asked.

'I thought he did. Lazarus believed he did. But why then didst he not come to help his beloved friend?'

Benjamin had no answer for this so he said nothing. The pitiful wailing of the mourners could still be heard from within the house and it was starting to depress Ben. He sighed deeply. This was all so sad, so miserable. Simeon buried his head in his hands and wept quietly. Ben began to feel embarrassed. Not knowing what to say or do. He decided to try and change the subject.

A woman came running towards the house. Her robes sailing in the wind behind her.

'Who's she?' Ben asked.

Simeon wiped his eyes and looked.

'Martha,' he answered. 'She was one of Lazarus' sisters.'

'Why is she running around like that?'

Simeon sighed with exasperation. 'Benjamin, dost thou think I knoweth all things?'

'Not at all,' replied Ben. 'I definitely don't think that.' This time it was Ben who shuffled a little further away from Simeon. They sat in silence like two stubborn mules, both enjoying this little verbal duel. Benjamin liked Simeon, he wasn't afraid to speak his mind and that was good.

The woman that Benjamin had seen sitting in the centre of the room suddenly ran out of the house and began racing toward the hills.

'I do not know,' said Simeon, anticipating Ben's next question.

'I wonder what she came rushing out of the house like that for,' said Benjamin.

'That was Mary, Lazarus' other sister. Lazarus is buried by the hills, perhaps she goeth there to mourn,' Simeon told him.

'Okay, now you're cooking! See you've got a good detective's brain,' teased Ben.

Simeon looked at Ben as if he had gone completely mad. 'My name is Simeon, not Kay. I do not cook and my brain is not defective.'

Ben grinned to himself.

People from the house had started to follow Mary.

'Come on Simeon, let's go as well,' said Benjamin.

'I can grieve for Lazarus here. I do not need to be at his grave.'

'Oh come on Simeon. I just want to see why that woman was in such a hurry.'

Evidently Simeon must have been a little curious too because he got up quickly and began to walk with Ben. Taking huge heavy strides, Simeon surged ahead, forcing Ben to jog a few paces after every two or three steps, just to keep up. When Benjamin jogged alongside him, Simeon began to run. With laughter he sprinted away from Ben. Benjamin began to run flat out, trying to catch up with Simeon but the boy could really move.

'Thou shalt not catch me, moron!' Simeon shouted over his shoulder as he sped away from Ben.

The cheek of Simeon catching on to the word, moron, was almost too much. 'I can't believe it,' said Ben to himself. 'I just got called a moron by a guy wearing a long dress and a pair of sandals.'

Seizing the challenge Ben began to run faster, he had to catch up with Simeon. Digging his heels in he raced up behind his challenger. Stretching out his hand Ben tried to grab him but Simeon seeing how close Ben was, simply stepped up a gear and ran faster.

'Run as fast as thou canst but thou wilt not catch me.'

'Who do you think you are, Simeon? The gingerbread man?' Ben yelled. He could run no further. Panting for breath he stopped and sat on the ground.

Seeing that Ben had given up, Simeon walked back to him. Gloating over his victory he sat beside Ben.

'Where did you learn to run like that?' Ben asked between gasps.

'Chasing sheep,' Simeon answered brightly.

'What, the turbo-charged variety?' Ben joked.

Again Simeon looked puzzled, but he sensed Ben was paying him a compliment and he smiled.

'Look!' Ben shouted. 'The teacher.'

Immediately the smile left Simeon's face and a scowl replaced it. 'He cometh too late. What use is he now?'

Mary was walking toward the teacher and when she reached him she fell to her knees. Benjamin went a few steps closer, trying to hear their conversation.

'If thou hadst been here, my brother would not have died,' she said.

'See!' whispered Simeon to Benjamin. 'I told you it was his fault.'

The teacher looked at Mary. He looked at Martha, he looked at the weeping crowd, and then he too began to cry.

'Thou canst see how much he loved Lazarus?' Simeon whispered. 'Surely if he had the power he would have come and saved his friend.'

The teacher asked where Lazarus was buried and the crowd led him to the site. Ben was expecting to see a freshly-dug grave in the earth, and a few flowers lying on it, but things were really different here. He could see a cave with a huge stone blocking the entrance.

'Take ye away the stone,' said the teacher.

Several people stepped back in amazement, gasping at the thought of what the teacher had asked them to do. Murmurings swept through the crowd like a forest fire. Tears fell from the teacher's eyes but he was silent, staring at the tomb before him. What did he think he was going to do?

Martha stepped forwards. She looked nervous. 'Lord, he hath been dead for four days, by this time there will be a bad smell.'

'Oh, gross!' Ben muttered under his breath. All around him people were covering their noses with their hands and clothing. Several men from the crowd gathered together and after some time, with their united strength, they managed to push the stone aside.

Benjamin squeezed his nostrils shut with his fingers. A hush fell over everyone as they waited to see what would happen. No one really wanted to be there when the stone was moved but nobody wanted to miss this either.

The teacher looked up to the sky and cried out, 'Father, I thank thee that thou hast heard me. I know that thou hearest me always: but I have said this so that these people may believe that thou hast sent me.' Then he shouted, 'LAZARUS, COME OUT.' His voice echoed around the hills. No one made a sound.

Benjamin stared into the darkness of the cave but he could see nothing. He strained his eyes, searching for some movement and then someone screamed. A man covered in bandages and cloths that were wound all around his body, shuffled slowly out of the cave. A few people from the crowd had run screaming down the hill but most people remained fixed to the spot, not daring to move until Martha suddenly ran forwards and with a shrill cry of delight, threw her arms around her brother.

'LAZARUS!' Shouts went up from everyone as Mary and Martha hurriedly began to free their brother from his grave clothes. People were dancing and singing. This was amazing. It was incredible. This was wonderful.

Pushing past the dancing crowd, Ben tried to reach the teacher. He must speak to him and now was a perfect opportunity.

'Excuse me, excuse me,' Ben said as he tried to get past. Why wouldn't they get out of the way? All at once Ben began to feel terribly tired, so tired that he could hardly take another step. What was wrong with him? He had never felt this tired before.

'I must talk to the teacher... I must see the teacher,' Ben mumbled. He felt faint and almost collapsed. He would have to lie down for a little while. If he could just sleep for five minutes he would feel refreshed. He was falling, wouldn't anybody help him? With breathtaking speed, Ben was suddenly gathered up into a sky bathed with purple, blue, green and silver colours.

*   *   *   *   *

'I must speak to the teacher.... I must speak to the teacher.'

'Why, what have you done?'

'Huh? Oh Mum!' Benjamin was lying on his doorstep again.

'Why do you have to speak to the teacher?' his mother asked. 'You were mumbling something just now about speaking to the teacher.'

'Oh, it's nothing, Mum. I just remembered that there was something I wanted to talk to my teacher about.'

'Well, can I help?'

'No, I don't think so Mum, but I bet Jake can. Can I go to church on Sunday?'

'Church?' asked his mother with surprise. 'Why? Who died?'

Benjamin grinned. 'Ever heard of Lazarus, Mum?'

Chapter 18

What did people wear to church these days? The last time Ben had been to church he had worn a frilly white christening gown and he couldn't wear that... it would never fit now. He decided to put on a pair of black jeans and a brand new white T-shirt.

'You're not going like that, are you?' His mother looked him up and down slowly. 'Shouldn't you be wearing a tie?'

'I haven't got one,' said Ben.

'That's no excuse, you can borrow one of your Dad's.'

'No way!' Ben was starting to feel very defensive. His mother had that determined look in her eye and he could see that she wasn't going to back down easily. 'I look all right like this, I'm not scruffy.'

'I never said you were, but -'

'Leave him Claire,' interrupted Ben's father. 'He looks fine. Come on, Ben, I'll give you a lift in the car, I want to go into the village and get a newspaper.'

'Thanks, Dad,' said Ben with surprise. It wasn't often that his father stuck up for him.

Standing outside the church building Ben hesitated.

He wanted to go inside but something was holding him back. He wasn't sure what it was but he'd almost decided to make his way home again when Melanie arrived.

'Hello, Ben,' she said cheerfully. 'Are you waiting for Jake? You'll have a long wait I'm afraid, church has only just started.'

'Yeah, I know. I'm going in. I decided to give it a try,' Ben said sheepishly.

'Excuse me,' said Melanie, 'but is the same Ben I met last week? Is this Ben - not if you paid me, over my dead body, you're a bunch of losers - Carpenter?'

Ben laughed. 'Yeah, that's me, I guess.'

Melanie smiled. 'I'm really glad you came. Come on you can sit with me.' Linking her arm through Ben's they walked together into the church.

Ben was stunned by the church. It wasn't anything like he had imagined it would be. About sixty or seventy people were inside. As Ben entered they began to sing. The words to the song were shown on an over-head projector and Ben found the tune catchy and easy to pick up. They sang about 'delighting yourself in the Lord.' Everyone sang with enthusiasm. A lady played the keyboards at the front and there was also a boy of about 18 or 19 playing the guitar. Ben noticed that several of the little children had tiny tambourines which they beat eagerly. Not a single child kept time with the music but no one seemed to mind. The song was repeated twice, which pleased Ben. This wasn't going to be as bad as he thought.

Three rows in front, sat Jake and Kate. When Kate turned around and saw Ben sitting with Melanie she opened her mouth wide with surprise and began whispering excitedly to Jake. Jake turned around and on seeing Ben he raised his hand and waved. Ben still felt embarrassed about turning up at church after his rantings at the festival.

An elderly man wearing a suit and tie stepped up to the front and began to give out some notices. 'If you're here with us for the first time today, we give you a very warm welcome,' he said.

Half of the young people in the church swung around and grinned at Ben. Melanie nudged him three times. Ben smiled, these were nice people.

'Is he the preacher?' Ben whispered to Melanie. He was referring to the old man.

'Who, Mr Edwards? No, he's our church secretary,' she replied. 'You know who our pastor is... it's Greg.'

Ben was shocked. Greg didn't look like a preacher. Mr Edwards looked like a preacher, even if he did smile a lot. Greg couldn't be a preacher... he was into basketball... he had little kids... he was into body-building, wasn't he? Perhaps he had misunderstood what Melanie said, after all she said that Greg was the Pastor. What was a Pastor? Maybe he was some sort of visiting youth worker.

'Melanie, what's a Pastor?' Ben asked.

'He's the leader of our church,' she answered.

Ben still wasn't satisfied with her answer. 'But who does the preaching?'

'Greg does,' Melanie told him.

'Well, well, well,' thought Benjamin to himself, 'life is full of surprises.' He still could not quite believe it when Greg stepped up to the front, opened his bible and began to speak.

'What would you think if I told you that right now there were some men on the roof of our building?' Greg asked. 'If you listen carefully, you can hear them walking about.' Everyone was quiet apart from the occasional nervous giggle. 'Suddenly,' said Greg, 'a hole starts appearing in our ceiling, right there, just above me.' Greg pointed to the ceiling. 'What's that? Hey look! I can see some men - what are they doing? They're lowering somebody down by some ropes.' Greg smiled at the congregation who were staring at the ceiling. 'Wouldn't that be a strange sight. You know, that actually happened when Jesus was preaching...'

Greg began to tell the story of how a group of men had been so desperate to get their paralysed friend to Jesus that they made a hole in the roof of the building where Jesus was speaking and lowered their friend down through it. The way Greg told the story made it exciting, especially the part where Jesus eventually healed the man. It sounded so much like something the teacher would do. Ben began to wish he could have been there, seen the look on the people's faces when a man suddenly crashed through the roof. Greg went on to tell them about Jesus having the power to forgive sins and it was at this point that Ben began to feel uneasy. Was Greg talking directly to him, reminding him of his bad language and fighting?

At the end of the meeting everyone sang another song and then Greg said that he would close in prayer. Everyone bowed their heads but Ben still felt silly. It made him feel so uncomfortable. After all they couldn't be sure that God was really listening.

Greg was standing at the door of the church when Ben was going out. 'Hey, Ben! Really good to see you.'

Ben was surprised that Greg wasn't sore about the way he had spoken to him at the basketball tournament.

'Has anyone invited you to the barbecue?' Greg asked.

'I was just going to,' said Jake.

'We've got a barbecue organised for the youth group at my house on Friday at 7 pm,' said Greg. 'I live along this road, number 3, the house with the red door. I'll drive you home when it's finished, if you like?'

'You can come, can't you, Ben?' Melanie asked him.

'Yeah, thanks. I'll be there,' said Ben. 'Greg, I erm... I'm sorry about the things I said at the tournament last week.'

He felt that he really must offer some sort of apology for his behaviour.

Greg smiled, 'Forget it, I already have. See you on Friday.'

Bradley and Simon walked up to Ben and chatted for a while. It seemed that everyone was going to this barbecue on Friday. Ben was really looking forward to it.

Having said his goodbyes, Ben began the long walk back to Village Heights. He had only gone a few yards when Melanie caught up with him.

'I think it took a lot of courage for you to come here today - especially after everything you said about church. But I'm really glad you decided to give it a try.'

Ben wished he didn't feel so tongue-tied around Melanie but she was so different from any of the girls at school. She was someone he really wanted to impress. As Ben walked home he wondered if Melanie had a boyfriend. She didn't seem to hang around with any boy in particular. He wondered if she liked him, she was very friendly toward him but she seemed to be that way with everyone. Maybe on Friday at the barbecue he would be able to get to know her better.

*   *   *   *   *

Instead of going straight home, Ben decided to walk an extra mile or so and go to the beach. He was hungry and his mother would have a steaming hot roast dinner on the table by now, but he had to find the stone again. The story Greg had told in church had given him a longing for another adventure. How wonderful it would be if Ben could be transported to the exact time and place where Jesus had healed the man who came through the ceiling. That had to be the work of the teacher.

Ben arrived at the beach, sat on his rock and waited for the stone to show itself. He didn't care how long it took, he wasn't budging until he found it.

It was late in the evening and growing dark when Benjamin finally admitted defeat, gave up and went home.Tears of frustration and disappointment stung his eyes. Having had only a small bowl of cornflakes for breakfast, he was now starving. He was also very tired, probably too tired to eat. Ben trudged on feeling sorry for himself. More than anything, he wanted to be home.

'Where on earth have you been?' Claire shouted when Ben walked in through the door.

His mother had been looking out of the window for him. His father sat at the table with a newspaper in front of him. It was open at the crossword page but Dan hadn't filled in any of the answers.

'Sorry,' said Ben. It was all he could manage.

'Oh no, sorry's not good enough,' said his father looking irate. 'I think you owe us an explanation. You've been gone all day and half the night. We've been worried sick.'

'Sorry,' Ben repeated.

His mother stepped toward him. 'Well? Where have you been?'

'I just went to the beach, that's all,' Benjamin answered.

'Just went to the beach?' exploded his father. 'We thought you were going to church.'

'I did go to church,' said Ben. 'I went to the beach afterwards.'

There was a heavy silence for a few seconds and then Dan slammed his fist on to the table. 'But you have to walk right past this cottage to get to the beach. Are you telling me that you walked right past here and didn't even bother to pop in and let us know where you were going?'

'Sorry,' said Ben. 'I didn't think I would be too long. I guess I lost track of the time.'

His father got up from his chair and walked angrily over to Ben. He stood directly in front of him, their noses almost touching. Ben wanted to take a step back but he knew that even the slightest movement might infuriate his father to even greater anger.

'Look at me, boy!' his father shouted. 'We wondered if you'd got into another fight and were lying in a ditch somewhere but no... oh no, you go swanning off to the beach without a single thought for anyone but yourself.'

'Oh, so it would be better for me to be lying in a ditch would it? You should be happy that I am home safely.'

His father raised his hand as if to slap Ben, but held back.

'Go to your room, Benjamin. Before I do something that you might regret.'

'Don't worry, I'm going,' said Ben. What a day! He was upset enough about not being able to find the stone, he didn't need all this aggravation from his parents.

Slamming the door behind him, he left the room and made his way upstairs.

The door was quickly opened again and his father shouted up at him, 'And you can forget about going out for the next week unless it's with us. You want to behave like a little kid, then you'll be treated like one.'

In his room Ben slumped to the floor and grabbed his hair in his hands. What was wrong with them? Surely they were over-reacting. How could they not let him go out for a whole week? What about the barbecue? 'Oh no,' Ben whined quietly, 'I'm really going to impress Melanie if I'm grounded.'

There was a soft tap on the door and Ben's mother entered carrying a sandwich and some hot chocolate on a tray.

'Here you are,' she said putting the tray on his bed. 'You must be starving, I don't think you've eaten all day, have you?'

'No, I haven't,' replied Ben. 'Thanks, Mum.'

His mother half smiled at him and seeing that she might be beginning to soften Ben tried to reason with her.

'Mum, he's not really going to ground me, is he? I've got to go to a barbecue on Friday.' His mother didn't say anything so Ben continued. 'It's at Greg's house. He's the leader of the church and he asked me to come. I already said I would.'

'Sorry, Ben, but I can't see your Dad changing his mind. We really have been very worried about you.'

'Please, Mum, can't you talk to him?'

'I don't think so, love,' she said. Leaving the room she closed the door gently behind her.

Chapter 19

By Thursday Ben was almost going out of his mind with worry. For four days he had been a shinning example of a helpful, obedient, even cheerful, son but his parents showed no signs whatsoever of changing their minds about his punishment. Whenever he raised the subject of the barbecue he would always get the same answer, 'Well, whose fault is it that you can't go?' They were sticking to their guns over this one. What hope did he have now?

On Friday morning Ben got up early and made breakfast for the family, as he had been doing all week. He even cut some roses from the cottage garden and placed them in a vase on the table. His mother loved fresh flowers, maybe she would appreciate his efforts. After breakfast he washed up the dirty dishes and hung the washing on the line.

When his mother suggested that they go for a drive and have a picnic at any suitable place they found, Ben made cheese and ham sandwiches to take. He was trying so hard to get into their good books but half of his efforts seemed to go unnoticed.

They ate their picnic by a lake, about ten miles away

from Westly point. His parents were in a good mood, relaxed and happy. Ben decided to give it one last try.

'Dad, I'm really sorry about last Sunday. I understand how it must have given you and Mum a scare. It was thoughtless of me not to tell you where I was going and I really am very sorry.'

'Well, Ben, that's good - I'm glad you've realised all that,' said his father. 'These are terrific sandwiches.'

'Dad, I was wondering if maybe -'

'No,' said his father.

'But you don't even know what I was going to ask,' Ben retaliated.

'Yes, we do, Ben,' said his mother. 'It's the same thing you've been asking about all week. You want to go to that barbecue.'

'Well, can I?'

'No,' said his father.

'But Dad why? I've tried to make it up to you, what more can I do?'

'Yes, Ben and you've done very well, but we said one week and that's how long you will be grounded for.'

'Whoever heard of being grounded on their holiday!' moaned Benjamin. 'Nobody gets grounded on their holiday!'

'Is that right?' said Dan. 'Well let's ring up the *Guinness Book of Records* and enter you as the first.'

*   *   *   *   *

It was almost five o'clock when they arrived back at the cottage. Just two hours left and that would be it, the barbecue would start without him. What could he do now? Time was running out fast and there were only so many good deeds a person could do in a day.

'Dad, we haven't been fishing yet and we've been here for nearly three weeks already. How about we go tomorrow? We could fish at the lake we were at today, lots of people seem to fish there.' Ben was frantically trying to win Dan over and offers to go on a father-and-son fishing trip might just do it.

'Fishing, eh?' said Dan.

'Yeah, just us two - no women allowed,' Ben grinned at his father. It was working, Dan was looking up at him with a glint in his eye. Ben held his breath and waited for his father's answer. The suspense was killing him. He must strike while the iron's hot.

'We haven't been fishing together for ages. Come on, Dad, you know how much you enjoy it.'

'Fishing, eh?'

'Just you and me, it'll be brilliant,' said Ben. He was carefully watching his father and desperately hoping that he would agree.

Dan suddenly wrinkled his nose, 'Mega boring,' he sang. He folded his arms and stared at the ceiling. He looked remarkably like Ben.

An explosion of laughter filled the room. This was a good sign.

'Dad...' said Ben when the laughter had died down.

'Yes, Ben.'

'Dad, please can I -'

'Yes, Ben.'

'Dad, please can I go to the barbecue tonight?'

'Ben,' said his father smiling, 'I said yes.'

Leaping into the air, Ben performed a variety of victory dances and gave his father a huge bear hug. 'Thanks, Dad,' he said.

'I'll be holding you to the fishing!' his father warned.

Ben beamed at him. 'No problem!' He ran up the stairs two at a time to shower and change his clothes.

After using some of his father's aftershave and a little of his mother's hair gel, Ben admired himself in the mirror. 'Hold on to your hat, Melanie,' he said to his reflection, 'I'm on my way.'

'Ben! Glad you could make it,' said Greg when Ben knocked on his door. 'Come on through, everyone's in the garden.'

Ben followed Greg through the house. His eyes immediately searched for Melanie but he couldn't see her anywhere. People were scattered all over the lawn and at the end of the garden, under a large weeping willow tree, Ben could see Jake talking to Bradley and Rick. He decided to join them.

'Hi, Ben,' Jake said. 'I hope you're hungry, Greg makes an amazing burger. We call them "bloaters", you'll find out why.'

Ben laughed. 'Where's Kate and Melanie?' he asked. He thought it would sound less suspicious if he asked after Kate as well.

'Oh you know what girls are like. They spend all day trying to decide what to wear. You should see Melanie's bedroom, there are clothes everywhere, it looks like she's having a jumble sale. I swear she's got the whole contents of her wardrobe out.'

'Only half my wardrobe actually,' said Melanie approaching them. Kate was with her.

'You look nice, Melanie,' said Ben.

'Thank you,' Melanie replied, throwing a superior look at her brother.

'Come on everyone, Gary's here now, so grab a chorus book and we'll have some songs while the barbecue's cooking,' shouted Greg.

The same boy that Ben had seen playing the guitar in church last Sunday was now strumming a few chords.

'Can we sing number 37?' called Melanie. 'It's my favourite, I love that one.'

Once again Ben felt at ease with these people. The singing was lively and fun but sometimes quiet and thoughtful. Some of the songs were about Jesus which made Ben think about the teacher. It was weird but the things these people were saying and singing, made it sound as if they actually knew the teacher. That wasn't possible, was it?

'Come and get it,' yelled Greg when the burgers were ready. Jake was right they were fantastic. Ben sat on the grass to eat and Melanie sat beside him, making him instantly nervous. He hoped he didn't have ketchup on his chin or lettuce stuck between his teeth.

'Enjoying yourself?' Melanie asked.

'Yeah it's great. Good food, good company, what more could a man ask for?'

Melanie smiled, 'I'm going to get a drink, want one?'

'Yes, thanks,' replied Ben, wishing that he had thought of offering to get a drink for her.

A tall boy aged about seventeen or eighteen came into the garden. He had long dark hair that was tied into a pony tail and he was wearing very expensive-looking clothes. In one hand he dangled his car keys and in the other he carried a mobile phone.

'Who's he?' Ben asked Jake.

Jake looked up and moaned quietly, 'Oh no, he's Marc Farringdon.'

'Don't you like him?'

'It's not that,' said Jake, 'he's always hanging around Melanie and he's far too old for her.'

'Oh, I see,' said Ben beginning to feel worried.

'Marc's family own half of this village and they give him anything he wants so he's used to getting his own way. He's been to a basketball training camp in America - which is why you haven't seen him before today,' explained Jake.

'He's a brilliant basketball player,' said Kate.

'He's not that good,' Jake said scowling at Kate.

Ben was beginning to dislike this Marc Farringdon person immensely.

'Don't look now, he's coming over,' whispered Jake. 'Try not to get on the wrong side of him, Ben, he's got a vicious temper.'

'All right Jake?' Marc said. 'Been looking after Melanie for me?'

Jake made some sounds that didn't really sound like either yes or no. 'This is Ben,' he said.

Marc looked at Ben. 'You just moved into the village?' He asked.

'No, we're here on holiday.'

'On holiday!' scoffed Marc. 'Don't tell me you've actually come to this snoring little village for a holiday.'

'Yes, we have,' said Ben with defiance. His temper was already beginning to rise. 'My mother is a well-known author and she's working on another book. She's come here to write, the peace and quiet is ideal for her.' This Marc character was seriously irritating him.

'I've just come back from the States,' bragged Marc.

Nobody said anything until Melanie came back with drinks for herself and Ben.

'I didn't know what you wanted so I chose Coke, okay?' said Melanie as she handed Ben his drink.

'Great, thanks,' said Ben taking it.

'Melanie,' said Marc, 'can I have a word?' He led Melanie to a quiet part of the garden.

Ben couldn't stop staring at them. What were they talking about? Marc had one hand resting on Melanie's shoulder, as he talked to her. She seemed to be really interested in whatever it was that he had to say. Relief swept through Ben when Greg asked everyone to sit in a circle. He was pleased when Melanie sat beside him again but not so pleased when Marc sat on the other side of her.

'There's still plenty of food left,' said Greg, 'so help yourselves to whatever you want. But I just thought it would be a nice idea if we could use this time for one or two of us to share their stories of how they came to know Jesus and came to have him living in their lives. Do we have any volunteers?'

Bradley raised his hand and soon began to tell everyone how devastated he was when his parents got divorced. He said how angry he was with them, especially when his Dad moved away to start a new life in Australia.

'I felt as though my Dad had just abandoned me, like I didn't matter to him any more and then one day when I was walking past the church I saw a poster outside saying, "Jesus said I will never leave you or abandon you". It was the first time I had ever thought about Jesus caring about me and I wanted to know more, so I started to come to church with Simon who I knew was already a Christian. It's not a very dramatic testimony but that's how my life changed. It was like Jesus was telling me that even though my Dad had left me, he would never ever do the same.'

Greg thanked Bradley and waited to see who would

want to tell their story next. When nobody volunteered Greg's wife asked if she could say something. She told them that she had become a Christian when she was fifteen years old and gave them a hilarious testimony about how she used to play games with Jesus by saying things like, 'Dear Jesus, I'll believe in you if you prove yourself to me by getting me a new pair of shoes by next Friday.' Sometimes she would get what she wanted and sometimes she wouldn't but she still continued to play those games until one day she heard something that was to change her life forever. 'I heard that Jesus once said "Blessed are they that believe in me even though they can't see me", and I realised that this meant I had to stop looking for proof of Jesus being there and start exercising faith. I had to start trusting God.'

Greg chose a few more choruses and then announced that there were strawberries and cream for anyone who wanted any.

'Oh Melanie, I almost forgot,' said Marc, 'I bought you a present while I was in the States. I'll just go and get it, it's in my car.'

Melanie blushed as Marc dashed away.

'Lucky old Melanie,' said Jake sarcastically.

Ben expected a quick retort from Melanie, but she was unusually quiet.

'Excuse me a moment,' she said to Ben, 'I'm just going to get some strawberries.'

Ben watched as Marc returned. He walked over to Melanie and gave her something in a yellow and white striped gift bag. Melanie peeped inside and pulled out a small pink teddy bear wearing a frilly dress. Together they walked back to where Ben, Jake and the others were sitting.

'Isn't it cute,' Melanie said showing the little bear to Kate. 'Thanks Marc, but you really shouldn't have.'

Ben couldn't bear to look at Marc's smug expression. There was an awkward silence for a while.

'Come on, who wants to go for a ride in my new car?' Marc asked.

'We can't,' said Jake, 'Greg is going to tell us how he became a Christian later on.'

'Don't let Greg tell you what to do; make your own decisions,' said Marc crossly.

'I am,' Jake replied, 'and I'm staying.'

'So am I,' said Melanie.

'Me too,' said Ben.

Marc suddenly turned and looked at Ben. 'Yeah? Well I wasn't asking you,' he snarled.

Ben was caught off guard. He could feel himself beginning to redden. He hadn't expected that, he wasn't prepared for it.

'Don't be so rude,' said Melanie. 'Ben's a guest amongst us.'

'Ahhh, isn't that cute, Ben's getting Melanie to stick up for him.'

Ben's anger had now peaked. He was ready to explode. He already had one black eye - what difference would another one make.

'Don't spoil the barbecue, Marc,' said Jake, trying to cool things down.

'What's wrong with Ben then? Cat got your tongue? Or do you only speak when Melanie says you can?' Marc wasn't going to let this go.

Ben felt his fists clench. He was just about to let loose a flying punch when he suddenly stopped. He wasn't quite sure why he stopped but he knew fighting wouldn't solve anything. Greg had laid on this outstanding barbecue so that he could share Jesus with everyone. Marc just wanted to ruin everything.

'Oh look, he's got his fists ready,' Marc jeered. 'Fancy having a fight do you?' He gave Ben a hard shove. 'Come on then, let's see what you're made of.'

'Listen you,' began Ben, 'don't start shoving me around and acting like a prize turkey. We all know you're a jerk - you don't have to prove it.'

Marc's face clouded over. He was almost purple but not from embarrassment, he was infuriated. Ben could see a small angry vein popping out on Marc's neck.

'Greg invited me here and I'm not going to ruin the evening for him.'

Marc laughed with contempt. 'Greg just lays on these barbecues so that he can get more people to come to his church. It's a publicity stunt that's all.'

'That's not true,' said Jake speaking up, 'he does it so that he can tell us about the love of God. He's actually doing us a favour.'

Marc sighed. 'Let me tell you something. Now this might come as a shock to you so brace yourself. Ready?... There is no Santa Claus, there is no Easter Bunny and most importantly of all, there is no God.'

Melanie ran over to Greg and asked to borrow his Bible.

'Oh don't start quoting the Bible at me, Mel,' Marc grumbled. 'I'll tell you now - the Bible has got absolutely nothing to say to me.'

'Oh I think you'll find it has,' she said flicking through the pages. 'Here we are: Psalm 14 verse 1. Perhaps Ben might like to read it to you,' she handed the Bible to Ben.

'Read it then,' Marc sneered, 'it won't make any

sense, the Bible never does.'

Ben looked at verse one and smiled. He cleared his throat. 'Now this may come as a shock to you, Marc, so brace yourself... Psalm 14 verse 1 says, "The fool says in his heart, 'there is no God'".' After a few seconds silence Kate sniggered. Soon everyone was roaring with laughter. Marc's mobile phone started ringing which for some reason added to the hilarity of the moment. Hoots of laughter went up as Marc took his call.

'Melanie,' said Marc irritably, 'a friend of mine from Ravenswood is having a party. Do you want to come or are you going to stay here with this lot?'

'I'm staying right here,' Melanie said. 'Good food, good company, what more could a girl ask for?' She winked at Ben as Marc stomped out of the garden with heavy strides.

'Was that Greg who brought you home?' Ben's mother asked when he floated in at 10.45 pm. 'You should have asked him in for a cup of coffee.'

'I did Mum, but he said he had to get back and help his wife clear up.'

'Enjoy yourself?' Dan asked.

'Yeah, it was really good.'

Ben couldn't stop smiling. It had been one of the best evenings of his life. Once he would have thought that not fighting would make him look weak and timid but in fact it had quite the opposite effect. Ben had kept his head and Marc was the one who ended up looking stupid.

Ben replayed the evening over and over in his head. After Marc had left, Melanie had stayed by Ben's side all evening, laughing at his jokes and telling him even better ones that had him in stitches. It had been a wonderful evening, especially towards the end when Ben had asked Melanie if she had a boyfriend. Melanie had blushed a little and then said, 'Well, that depends.'

'Depends on what?' Ben asked.

'You.' Melanie said shyly and then grinned.

With unfortunate timing Greg had then come over to Ben to offer him a lift home, but that was okay. Melanie had hinted quite heavily that she liked Ben which had been a perfect end to a lovely evening.

'Earth to Benjamin, come in Benjamin.' Ben's father was trying to get his attention. 'Will you stop staring into space and please stop smiling - what are you doing, rehearsing for a toothpaste commercial?'

'Sorry,' said Ben still smiling. 'I'll go to my room, I'm a bit tired.'

'Want some hot chocolate?' asked his mother.

'No thanks, mum, I'm fit to burst.' Ben patted his stomach.

'Don't forget we're fishing tomorrow,' said his father.

'Yeah, but only if you behave yourself,' said Ben closing the door as he left the room.

'Well something's certainly put a smile on his face,' said Dan to his wife.

'Something or someone,' said Claire.

Dan sighed, 'Ahh young love. Do you know, I can still remember the first time I kissed you, we were standing outside the maths block at school, you were 15 and I was 16... See Claire, I can be romantic. I bet you never thought I would remember that.' He beamed at his wife proudly.

Claire looked disappointed, 'It wasn't outside the maths block, it was on the park bench,' she said tutting.

'No it wasn't.' Dan was adamant. 'It was definitely outside the maths block.'

'Oh yes!' Claire laughed nervously. 'Of course, you're right. I was confusing you with someone else.' She left the room quickly to make a hot drink.

Dan followed her into the kitchen. 'Claire,' he said, his voice taking on a mock serious tone, 'I think you've got some explaining to do.'

Chapter 20

Tea was already on the table when Ben and his father returned from their fishing trip. Full of stories about 'the one that got away', their cheerful chatter continued throughout the meal.

'Did you get much writing done while we were out?' Dan asked his wife.

'Yes, tons,' she replied. 'Tomorrow I shall have a day off from writing. I'd really like to go to an antique fair in Downshall Village.'

Dan agreed heartily. 'Fine, we'll make a day of it.'

'But tomorrow's Sunday,' said Ben.

'Yes and the day after that is Monday,' said his mother teasing, 'aren't you a clever boy.'

'No, I'm serious Mum. I have to go to church tomorrow.'

'Well, you can go next Sunday. The church isn't going anywhere but the antiques fair only comes round once in a blue moon,' she said.

'Please Mum, it was really interesting last week. I'd like to go again.'

His mother shook her head as she chewed her food.

'Sorry Ben - we're going to the fair and that's final. Right Dan?' She looked to her husband for support.

'No arguments whatsoever,' he said giving Ben a stern look.

The relaxed atmosphere left the table after that and a stiffness entered their conversation.

Claire tried to make light of it. 'Most kids wouldn't go to church if they were giving out £5 notes and here's our son pleading to go.'

'Yeah, well maybe most kids have never tried it. It's not like you'd expect,' said Ben trying not to raise his voice.

Dan decided to quickly change the subject. 'A man at the lake said the best place to fish is at a place called Old Harbour. Apparently it's not too far from here. I'll have to look it up on the map. Fancy a trip out there on Monday, Ben?'

Ben shrugged his shoulders. 'Don't mind,' he said flatly.

*   *   *   *   *

It was Tuesday before Ben had any time to himself and he knew exactly what he was going to do with it. He had been itching to get back to the beach and look for the stone again. It had been twelve days since his last adventure, now he was ready for more. With confident strides, he began the familiar trek to the sea.

Stepping on to the cold pebble beach, Ben saw the stone straight away. Kneeling beside it, he lifted it into his hands and waited. Like a tin can to a magnet, he was plucked up by the wind and sent flying into the vigorously spinning sky.

When Ben awoke he was immediately afraid. Something was wrong. He wasn't in a boat or sitting on a dusty road. He wasn't in a house and neither was he being poked in the ribs by a small child with a stick. He was completely alone and surrounded by darkness. This had to be a mistake, he shouldn't be here. Maybe he was lost in time. Maybe this was the end.

The fear in him began to rise. His imagination was starting to run riot. He was sure he could hear someone creeping up on him and what was that over there? Ben began to cringe away from hallucinatory bats. He ran from shadowy phantoms. This was crazy. Petrified he began to run, hoping to find someone, a light, a house, anything. Blinded by the darkness he ran full tilt into a large tree.

The impact of the collision propelled him backwards and threw him to the ground. Not quite sure what had hit him, Ben lay there as if dead. Scared out of his wits he began to scream for help. He knew it was childish to be afraid of the dark but who was looking? With a mixture of alarm and relief Ben was almost certain he could hear voices. Yes, he definitely could. Men's voices - maybe three or four of them. Instinctively Ben shrunk away. Who were these men? They could be a group of desperadoes looking for someone to pounce on and rob. What would they do when they discovered that Ben had no money? They might beat him up and leave him for dead.

Blood began pounding in Ben's ears. What should he do? Should he throw himself at the mercy of these men or keep perfectly still until they went away? He could see three men now, the moon had come out from behind a cloud and was casting a silvery glimmer of light over them.

117

They were big men, they could easily over power him.

Ben peered out from behind the bush. The men were were sitting together, talking quietly. With surprise, Ben discovered that he recognised them. They were the one's who had been in the boat that day the teacher had been walking on the water... and wasn't that Peter there?

Ben couldn't quite hear what they were saying so he crept a few yards closer and hid behind an even pricklier bush.

'We must pray. The teacher is over there and we shouldst keep watch,' said one of the men.

'This very night he told us that his soul was over-whelmed with sorrow to the point of death.'

Ben was baffled by this information. What could possibly frighten the man who had touched the face of a leper without even flinching?

The men bowed their heads and began to pray, each one murmuring quietly.

It looked as though Peter and the others had fallen asleep. Hold on a minute, Ben thought to himself, aren't they supposed to be keeping watch? Shrugging his shoulders he fumbled around in the darkness, hoping to see the teacher. He had only gone a little way when he heard someone talking. As Ben drew closer still, he was surprised to see the teacher alone. He was lying flat out on the floor, his head resting on his clenched fists. He was praying, 'Father if Thou art willing, take this cup from me.'

'What cup?' whispered Ben to himself. What did the teacher mean by that? Why should he be getting so upset about a cup?

'Yet not my will but Thy will be done.'

Wiping the sweat from his brow, the teacher got up

and made his way swiftly to where his men were meant to be praying and keeping watch. Ben followed a few paces behind, captivated by this amazing man.

When the teacher saw Peter and the others sleeping he groaned aloud. Peter stirred and on seeing the teacher, he nudged his friends awake.

'So thou couldst not keep watch for one hour.' The teacher looked hurt and Peter looked ashamed. 'Thou must pray,' he told them, 'the spirit is willing but the flesh is weak.'

Peter nodded and bowed his head in prayer. The teacher walked quickly back to the spot where he had been before.

Keeping a safe distance behind, Ben followed him. Kneeling down, the teacher closed his eyes and clasped his hands tightly together. He prayed silently, mouthing the words. Even though Ben couldn't hear anything, he could sense urgency and seriousness. The teacher's face twisted in agony. Huge drops of sweat fell from his forehead, like drops of blood. Ben began to feel frustrated and helpless. What could be so terrible that it would cause the teacher to be in such torment? Running into the darkness again, Ben tried to make his way back to Peter and the others but suddenly he was lost. Had they moved somewhere else or did Ben run in the wrong direction? He thought he could see a light shining ahead of him and ran towards it.

'Put out your lantern, we will be seen!'

A group of men stood plotting in the darkness.

'The one I kiss is the man, seize him,' said a nervous-sounding voice.

Ben crept just a little closer to see better. He vaguely recognised one of them as the teacher's friend. Ben had seen him around a few times. From out of the shadows a whole crowd of men and soldiers joined them. Each man carried a sword or a weapon of some sort. There were so many people there that Ben didn't think anyone would notice him if he mingled amongst them.

The man Ben recognised, stepped out into the darkness. Where was he going? He walked over to Peter and the other men. The teacher was back with them. With great terror, Ben watched as the man leaned forward and kissed the teacher on the cheek.

'That is the sign!' yelled another man.

'Now, men!' shouted the leader and the crowd surged forwards running, roaring and waving their weapons in the air.

'NO!' screamed Benjamin. 'STOP IT!' He watched, mesmerised, as the men advanced towards the teacher.

'So, Judas, thou wouldst betray me with a kiss,' said the teacher sadly.

The soldiers grabbed him roughly, pushing him to the ground, even though he wasn't struggling to get free. Ben was really angry now, how dare they treat the teacher like this.

'Leave him!' shouted Peter trying to push the soldiers away. Ben saw a glint of silver and watched as Peter, in his despair, raised his sword into the air. With remarkable precision his sword swooped down and struck someone on the side of the face, slicing off their ear. A piercing, high pitched scream filled the air.

The noises of the men shouting, the angry faces, the pushing and shoving, the screaming and the blood, all started to fade into the distance. Ben felt his legs crumbling beneath him. He was so dizzy now. His legs couldn't support him for a second longer. Benjamin fainted.

Chapter 21

When Ben came to, it was still dark, but not as dark as it had been. He was lying face down on a hill.

Ben was very thirsty. He sat up and looked around him. He was surrounded by people who were crying quietly. Was it day or evening, Ben couldn't be certain. The sky was dusky with the peculiar type of darkness that sometimes comes with a very bad storm. He looked at a small group of women standing a little way in front of him. He thought he recognised one of them. Wasn't that the woman Benjamin had met on his first adventure, the woman who was looking for her son? What was she looking at? Come to think of it, what were they all looking at? Ben turned around to see what was behind him.

'NO!' he shouted. 'NO! NO... WHY?'

There behind him were three large wooden crosses. On each cross a man was hanging, but there in the middle, was the teacher. Huge metal spikes had been banged into his hands and feet. He had a ring of thorns digging into his head, piercing his skin and sending tiny rivers of blood travelling along his face and dripping on to his body. He didn't even look like the same man. His face was twisted in pain, distorted by agony. Ben stared open-mouthed at the teacher's hands which were covered in blood, crushed, broken hands that had once brought healing and were filled with power.

The ground began to tremble. People screamed with fear. The teacher summoned up his last dregs of energy and cried out in a loud voice, 'Father, into Thy hands I commit my spirit.' The sky rumbled in anger and with a loud ripping sound, a flash of white lightning covered the earth, followed by a booming thunderclap.

'No!' Benjamin sobbed hysterically. Never had he seen such an awful sight, such cruelty. This man had done nothing to deserve this. Did the teacher know this was going to happen, is that what he was praying so urgently about?

The other people standing around the cross began wailing. Some men were holding back the woman that Ben had seen before, was she Mary?

An army officer, standing watching, spoke almost in a whisper, 'Surely, he was the Son of God.'

*   *   *   *   *

'Ben, get up from there. What on earth are you doing?'

His mother was standing at the door of the cottage and there he was again, lying on the doorstep. Ben stood up slowly.

'What's the matter? You've been crying.'

He didn't answer her but walked inside. With a heart as heavy as lead there was no way he could put a brave face on, even for his parents. So many angry questions raged inside his mind but he couldn't bring himself to think about any of them. All he wanted to do now was mourn. Sadness overwhelmed him.

'Ben!' His mother caught him by the arm. 'What is it, darling? What's happened?'

Shaking his head slowly, Ben shrugged his shoulders. He couldn't even bring himself to speak. With his head held low he made his way up to his room.

Sleep did not come easy that night. Ben's dreams were haunted by the sight of the teacher dying on the cross, the life being slowly sapped from his body, his face crushed and ashen, weary with torture and pain. Apparently Ben must have cried out in his sleep because his parents had come scurrying into his room in the early hours of the morning, telling him that he was having a bad dream.

All eyes were on Benjamin during breakfast. He could see his parents casting worried looks at him, trying to make cheerful conversation with him.

'We thought we'd all take a walk down to that little beach you're so fond of,' said his father.

Ben didn't respond.

'How about it then, Ben?' his mother asked him. 'Fancy showing us around your beach?'

Shaking his head, Ben picked up a slice of toast and nibbled the corner of it. He didn't feel like eating but his mother was watching him like a hawk.

'I'll pack sandwiches, and I made a fruit cake yesterday, we could take that.'

'No thanks,' said Ben. He didn't even look at her.

'Oh we can't go without you,' she said watching him carefully.

Tears began to well up in Ben's eyes and he was cross with himself for showing them this weakness.

'Just go will you. I'll be all right, I'm 14 not 4.'

It was quiet in the cottage after Dan and Claire left. They had packed a lunch for themselves and set off reluctantly without their son. Neither of them knew what had happened to upset Ben so much but Claire had her ideas.

'I'm sure he's broken up with Melanie, poor love,' she said.

'I don't know,' said Dan. 'I think Ben would have told us if he had a girlfriend.'

'It's girl trouble, Dan. You can see it a million miles away and besides, I can't think what else could have distressed him so much.'

*   *   *   *   *

Sitting on the rocking chair in his room, Ben stared at a dirty mark on the carpet. There was more than just girlfriend problems troubling him. Tears fell from his eyes. He wiped them away roughly. This was stupid. He didn't even know the teacher. He'd never managed to talk to him but he knew now who he was. He was the same Jesus that Jake and the others talked about. He was Jesus, the Son of God... but he was dead. Ben had seen it for himself. Why did everyone in that Church carry on as if nothing had happened? Why didn't Greg scream out about the inhumane way in which Jesus was killed?

A knock at the cottage door broke Ben's train of thought. Getting up he wiped his eyes once more and walked sorrowfully down the stairs to the door.

'Hello, Ben, where did you get to on Sunday? You said you would come to church again.'

Jake, Melanie and Kate were standing at the door smiling.

'Come in if you want,' said Ben not bothering to answer their question or make any effort to sound glad to see them.

They followed Ben into the cottage and sat down in the living room.

'I waited for you outside the church, I thought we could go in together as we did last week,' said Melanie.

'Yeah, well, I didn't want to go,' said Ben. He decided not to bother telling them about the antiques fair that he had been forced to go to.

'But Ben, you seemed to really like it and you sounded so enthusiastic at the barbecue, what happened?' Kate asked gently.

Ben remained silent for a while, his anger building slowly inside of him.

'You missed a brilliant talk on Sunday about Jesus being crucified on the cross,' said Jake.

'Oh yes! It was really good,' Melanie agreed. 'I never knew the part about the spear -'

'What spear?' Ben interrupted.

'Well after Jesus had died one of the soldiers got a spear and plunged it into Jesus' side. Blood and water came pouring out of him.'

A sharp pang of misery hit Ben somewhere in the middle of the chest. 'Why didn't he save himself. He could have done something to stop it from happening, couldn't he?' Ben asked.

'He had to do it, Ben,' said Jake. 'It was part of God's plan to save us.'

'Us? What do you mean, us? Don't drag me into this!' Ben shouted. 'I had nothing to do with it.'

Melanie looked surprised by Ben's outburst. 'Yes, you did, Ben, we all did.'

Ben turned on Melanie, how dare she suggest that it had anything to do with him. 'Marc was right, there is no God. Maybe Jesus was something special once, but now he's dead.'

'But Ben he -'

'Don't try and change facts with fancy words, Melanie. He's dead!'

'Ben, you don't have to get angry with Melanie,' said Jake softly.

'I'm not angry with her!' shouted Ben. 'But you people have to realise that he died. He really died.'

'But Ben -' Jake began.

'No, I won't listen to any buts. He is dead. Now if you don't mind I'd prefer it if you all left.'

Melanie looked hurt as she got up to leave. 'Come on, we'd better go,' she said.

Chapter 22

'Well, what did you think of it?'

Dan and Ben looked cautiously at each other and then smiled.

'It was brilliant, Claire.'

'Yeah, Mum, that was definitely the best book you've ever written.'

Claire breathed a sigh of relief. Over the last two days she had read aloud her entire new book.

'You must be the best writer in the world,' said Dan. 'I'm sure your editor will love it.'

'Dan! Don't exaggerate,' Claire laughed. 'Oh Ben, I've just realised, you forgot to go to church yesterday.'

Ben's bright expression changed. He frowned. 'I'm not going there any more.'

'Oh, aren't you?' Claire asked innocently.

'No. I don't have to go, do I?'

'Of course not,' Claire said.

Ever since Melanie had told him about the soldiers stabbing the teacher with a spear Ben had hardly been able to think of anything else.

Claire looked at Dan who said, 'Ben can we have a

chat? We're a bit worried about you and -'

'Later, Dad, if that's okay. I'm just going out for a walk.'

Ben had to escape. He couldn't bear all the questions he knew his parents were longing to ask him. He knew he'd been really moody and had hardly left the house these last few days, but he was hurting. If Jake and the others had seen what Ben had witnessed they would have known there was no way the teacher could have survived the cross. He was dead.

Finding the stone was easy. Ben could see shafts of silver light shooting up from among the pebbles. He watched it for a while but didn't touch it. What was the point? He might be transported to the scene of the cross again. He might actually see the soldier stabbing the spear into the teacher's side. Turning slowly, Ben began to walk away. Sea gulls circling overhead screeched loudly, as if they didn't want him to leave. One of the birds even swooped down and flew around Ben's head. 'Get lost!' he shouted brushing his ear with his hand. It reminded him instantly of the man who had lost his ear. No wonder Peter had struck him with the sword. He was trying to save the teacher from the horror of the cross. Poor Peter, how he must have grieved when the teacher was killed.

Why was it so cold all of a sudden? Ben folded his arms around his body, trying to keep warm. It was getting dark too. Looking up, Ben noticed that the birds had gone and that the beach was desolate. The darkness created a bleak atmosphere but it matched Ben's mood well. Something strange was in the air.

Without realising that he was doing it, Ben wandered over to the stone. Looking at it now, Ben felt nothing but anger and bitterness.

'He's dead, you lump of dumb rock!' he shouted. His voice echoed across the beach. He's dead... He's dead...' With a cry of rage Ben kicked the stone as hard as he could, wishing he could kick it into the depths of the sea, never to be seen again. As his foot made contact with the little rock, he was suddenly hauled upside down and into a frantically spinning, multicoloured sky. 'Stop!' he screamed into the mayhem. 'I don't want to go. I didn't want this!'

*   *   *   *   *

Rubbing his head Ben awoke. Oh no, what was he doing here? He could see a group of men sitting around a table.

It was Peter and the other men that were always with the teacher. There was tension in the air. Each man's expression was taut with anxiety, revealing just how frightened they were.

Speaking in low whispers, their voices sounded nervous, their conversations were jumpy.

'Be still, Peter, we must think,' said one of the men. Peter stood up and restlessly paced the room.

Ben wondered if he should come out of hiding and talk to them, but then again, maybe he was in the best place - these guys were scared!

'I heard something!' One of the men leapt from his seat and ran to the door, checking that it was locked. It was.

'Be calm, Thomas. The door is bolted and we must decide what we are to do.'

Peeping out from his hiding place, Ben could just see Thomas. He was looking at the door, his eyes staring at it in terror. It was peculiar to see such a big, strong looking man tremble with fear.

'We shouldst not be here, we should get out of Jerusalem. They killed the teacher and they will kill us too,' Thomas ran his hands worriedly through his hair.

The other men were silent, each one knowing that what Thomas said was true.

'After all that Jesus said, after all that he didst do before our very eyes - he just leaves us,' said Thomas, his voice faltering as he struggled to speak. 'We loved him... I loved him and now he is gone.' Burying his head in his hands he began to cry, his shoulders shaking with grief.

'Thomas, we told you, Jesus is not dead,' said one of the men. Why dost thou not believe us? He was here, in this very room. We touched him and spoke with him. If thou hadst been here thou wouldst have seen him but you stayed away.'

What on earth were they talking about? How could the teacher be alive?

'He was raised by the power of our mighty God. Believe us Thomas, we have seen him. Many people have seen him!'

'I cannot believe that,' Thomas said sadly.

'Neither can I,' said Ben to himself with equal sadness.

'We saw his hands and the nail marks,' said one of the men. 'He showed us his feet and his side.'

'Well, unless I see the nail marks in his hands and put my hand on his side, I will not believe it.'

Every man in the room looked at Thomas. Pity filled their eyes. Ben was beginning to feel very uncomfortable in his cramped position. He longed to stretch his arms and legs. The silence in the room was heavy. Ben wished they would all start talking again so that he could scratch his nose without worrying about the noise any movement might make.

'Peace be with you.'

The men leapt to their feet, Thomas included. Cries of, 'Lord' and 'Master' came excitedly from them. What was going on now? Ben couldn't see past Thomas.

'Thomas,' said a voice, 'put thy finger here, see my hands. Touch my side. Stop doubting and believe.'

Who was that? It certainly sounded like the teacher but how could it be? How did he get in? Nobody had opened the door, it was still heavily bolted.

Thomas fell to his knees. 'My Lord and my God,' he said looking down in shame and awe.

It was him! It was the teacher. 'Yes!' Ben whispered. This was the biggest miracle of them all. The teacher placed a gentle hand on Thomas' shoulder and Ben winced when he saw the horrendous wound mark on his hand.

'Because thou hast seen me, thou believeth. Blessed are those who have not seen me and yet believe.'

Wasn't that something that Greg's wife had said? She said we had to stop looking for proof of Jesus' existence and have faith.

Thomas nodded in agreement. He had only believed that Jesus was alive because he had seen it with his own two eyes but people like Jake, Melanie and Greg believed even though they couldn't see, that was what the teacher was saying wasn't it?

Ben wanted to get out there and join them. In his haste to get out of his hiding place, he lifted his head and cracked it hard against the wall. The room immediately became dark and then started to swirl, slowly at first and then with growing rapidity.

'Typical,' Ben groaned softly to himself as he was swept up into its current. No longer was he haunted by the sight of the teacher's broken body hanging lifelessly on the cross. Jesus was alive again! His sorrow had been swept aside the second he saw the teacher and although Ben didn't understand too much about it all, he somehow knew that this was reason to celebrate.

Chapter 23

How on earth did I get here?

Confusion filled Ben's mind as he looked around him. He was sitting on the basketball court in the village. Filled with exhilaration Ben suddenly remembered that the teacher was alive and he looked around for someone to share this wonderful news with but the place was deserted. The court was empty, apart from a red and purple basketball laying in the centre. Jumping to his feet Ben ran to the ball, bounced it a few times and did some fancy dribbling, working the ball around his legs. Today he could conquer the world. Today he could take on Orlando Magic single handed.

'Alive! Alive! Alive!' Ben chanted with each bounce of the ball. Driving up to the basket he leapt from the ground, taking the ball up with his right hand and shouting at the top of his voice, 'HE'S ALIVE!' Vigorously he slammed the ball into the net and caught the iron hoop with his hands. Dangling from the rim he drew his knees up to his chest and laughed loudly.

'How on earth did you do that? You slam dunked it.' Greg was clapping slowly in amazement. 'I just came to collect the ball. You actually slam dunked it!'

Ben released his hold and fell on his feet to the ground. 'Greg, I've got to talk to you.'

'Fire away, I'm all ears,' Greg led Ben to the side of the court where they sat down. 'Okay, what's up?'

'Well, I found out that Jesus died on the cross and I guess I thought that was the end but it wasn't was it?'

'No, actually it was only the beginning.'

Ben grinned, 'Yeah, that's what I figured - but why did he have to die in the first place, what was the point?'

Greg appeared thoughtful for a moment and then he answered. 'When God made this world, He made it perfect. There was no hatred, no fighting, no wars, there was even no death. He made man so that he would never die but then sin came into the world and ruined man's friendship with God. Because people had sin in their lives they were cut off from God. We are born sinful. You see no one is perfect, even little babies know how to do things wrong - no one has to teach them. So if man is sinful and God is Holy how can the two of them be friends again?'

Ben shrugged his shoulders. 'I don't know.'

'Well God made a plan to save people. He wanted to be friends again so He sent His Son, Jesus to die on the cross for us. When Jesus died He was punished for all our sins, including yours and mine.'

'But that's not fair is it? Jesus didn't do anything wrong.'

'You're right, it's not fair but that's what makes it so wonderful. Jesus was perfect and yet He was willing to take the blame for all the bad things we have done.'

'But I still don't get it, Greg. How does His dying save me?'

'Well the Bible tells us that everyone who believes in

Jesus and calls on His name has the right to be called a child of God. When Jesus spoke about how to get to heaven he said, "I am the way... no one comes to the Father except through me". Jesus has already paid the price of sin. If you were to die right this very second you would not be able to get into Heaven, simply by saying... I've been a good person, or sorry about all the bad things I've done - I didn't mean it. The only way you can get into Heaven is through Jesus. You have to say, I know that Jesus died for me and took the blame for all the bad things in my life and because of him I can be forgiven... but you have to believe that, Ben.'

Ben looked thoughtful. 'Are you telling me that all I have to do is believe?'

'That's what I'm saying, but there's something else that is very important. You have to be really sorry and ask Jesus to forgive you. Jesus often talked about repenting, and that means a complete turning away from the bad things in your life and asking him to give you strength to only do the things that please him.'

'What happens if I foul up?' Ben was worried. He didn't think he would be able to be good for the rest of his life, he was sure he would do some things wrong.

'Don't worry - you will, and when you do Jesus says that if we tell him what we have done wrong and say sorry - then He will forgive us.'

'But I am sorry,' said Ben.

Greg smiled, 'Well you're half way there then. Maybe you should talk to Jesus.'

Ben grinned, 'I've actually been trying to do that for some time now.'

'He's listening now, I promise you.'

Ben coughed a few times, 'I'm not sure I know what to say.'

'Just say what's in your heart,' encouraged Greg. 'Tell him how sorry you are for all the years that you shut him out of your life.'

'Okay.' Ben closed his eyes and bowed his head. He didn't care if anyone could see him, he was going to speak to the teacher at last. Maybe now, the teacher could be his friend. From what Ben had seen, Jesus changed the lives of all the people He touched, maybe Ben's life would change too. He wanted the same happiness that Jake, Melanie and the others had. Coughing again, Ben cleared his throat and began to pray.

'Jesus, Son of God, this is Benjamin, son of Daniel.'

Chapter 24

Benjamin arrived outside the church early on Sunday morning. He couldn't wait to see the look on Melanie and Jake's faces when he told them that he was a Christian now. Ben liked to think of himself as one of Jesus' followers. He had been speaking to Jesus every day in prayer and Greg had loaned him a small New Testament to read. The reports about Jesus were captivating, especially the miracles that He had done. Ben had even come across a part about Peter chopping off the man's ear. His name was Malchus. Reading on he learned that Jesus had touched and immediately healed him. 'What a pity,' Ben joked. He spent the rest of the day wondering whether that event had changed Malchus' life. Surely he must have believed Jesus was the Son of God after that.

'Ben, we heard the brilliant news!' Jake and Melanie were walking toward him.

'You did?' Ben was disappointed, he wanted to tell them himself.

'Yeah, Greg said you dunked the ball.'

'Did Greg say anything else?'

'No,' said Jake. 'Why, was there something else?'

Suddenly Ben was at a loss for words. He had imagined telling them all week but now it came to the crunch... 'I gave... I said... I erm... Well, I asked Jesus to be in my life.'

'You became a Christian!' Jake's eyes were wide open with surprise.

Ben smirked. 'Yeah. I'm a Christian.'

'Ben, that's fantastic!' Melanie hugged him.

'It won't always be easy, Ben. Sometimes the road gets rough but you'll always have Jesus there with you,' Jake told Ben, patting him affectionately on the back.

Singing the choruses with particular enthusiasm, Ben meant every word he sang. He had a new life. He had a new friend. He was a new person. After the service, Ben told the others about becoming a Christian. A flurry of excited people gathered around him.

'What did your parents say about it?' Melanie asked.

'I haven't actually told them yet,' Ben admitted.

'You should tell them,' said Jake. 'The Bible tells us that if we confess with our mouths and believe with our hearts that God raised Jesus from the dead, then we shall be saved. It'll be a big step but God will bless you for it.'

Ben nodded. 'You're right. I'll tell them tonight.'

*   *   *   *   *

In fact it was Wednesday before Ben could build up enough courage to tell his parents what had happened to him. They sat listening intently. He told them everything - from the very first adventure.

'The truth is, I'm not quite sure what happened to me out on the beach but I know that the teacher, er Jesus, was trying to show me who He really is and now that I know what He did for me on the cross... I can't turn my back on him ever again.' He stopped talking and looked at his parents, waiting for their reaction.

Dan sighed and stretched his arms above his head. 'I must admit, that was one heck of a story. I don't know what to say. What do you think, Claire?'

'Amazing,' Claire said thoughtfully.

'Look, don't say anything just now but come to church with me on Sunday and hear about Jesus for yourselves,' Ben said.

'Oh, I don't know about that,' said Dan looking shifty.

'Please, Dad. For me?'

'We can't Ben, we're going home early on Sunday morning,' his mother reminded him.

A lump rose in Ben's throat. He had experienced the most amazing adventure that had changed his life forever. Going home would be a real wrench.

'Well, we could pack our things, go to church and then drive home straight afterwards,' said Dan eventually.

'Excellent!' Ben beamed at his parents. 'I'm just going for a walk,' he told them.

'Mind if I tag along too?' his father asked.

Ben grinned, 'You can come, but only if you promise to hold my hand the whole time... I don't want you running off.'

'Get out of here!' Dan laughed, pushing his son playfully out of the cottage door.

They walked slowly to the beach. Ben knew that the stone was gone forever but that was okay. He had Jesus with him now, that was all that mattered.

'So this is the beach where you found the stone,' his father said.

'No, Dad,' Benjamin said thoughtfully. 'This is the beach where I found Jesus.'

* * * * *

On Sunday morning, Greg spoke about the power of Jesus that can change lives. He told them about a man in the Bible called Paul who persecuted Christians and had them thrown into prison and tortured. This very man met Jesus on the road to Damascus. It changed his life so much that he became one of the most powerful preachers ever. Ben looked at his parents. They were listening carefully to every word Greg was saying. Maybe there was hope for them.

After the service Greg came over to chat to Dan and Claire. Ben went to say goodbye to Melanie.

'Ben, I can't believe you're going already. I'm going to miss you.' Melanie held Ben's hand gently.

'I'd like to write to you - if that's okay,' Ben said.

Melanie smiled broadly. 'I'd like that very much. Come outside, Jake's got something for you.'

Outside, Jake stood waiting, along with the rest of the Eagles basketball team. 'We all chipped in to buy you this,' he said, handing Ben a package wrapped in blue paper. 'Anytime you want to come back and play for the Eagles, you'll always be welcome.'

'Yeah, especially now that you can dunk it!' Ricky laughed.

'Thanks,' said Ben, genuinely surprised that they had bought him a gift.

'Oh, I got you something too,' said Melanie. She handed Ben an enlarged photograph of them all, taken at the festival. 'That's so you don't forget us.'

'No chance,' said Ben, smiling at her. 'I've got something for you too.' Ben walked over to his father's car and grabbed the huge orangutang that he had won. He carried it over to Melanie.

'Oh, thanks! I'll treasure him forever,' she said.

'Yeah, well make sure you show it to Marc and tell him that I thought you deserved more than just a tiny teddy.'

Everyone laughed and Melanie hugged Ben tightly.

'See that, Dan?' Claire whispered urgently to her husband as they approached Ben.

'Well, have you said your goodbyes?' Dan asked Ben.

'Yes. I'm ready to go.'

'Oh, and Ben,' said his father, 'maybe next year, we can go to Florida.'

Ben looked disappointed and Dan laughed.

'Or maybe we could come back to Snooze Village?'

'Yes!' Ben hugged his father.

'Thanks, Mr Carpenter!' Melanie hugged him too. It took Dan completely by surprise.

'Get away, you pair of loonies,' he chuckled.

Ben ran over to Greg. 'Greg, we're going now. I just wanted to say thanks and I'll see you next year.'

'Wonderful,' said Greg. 'I'm really pleased. We'll get you to play for the Eagles again. Make sure you find a good church to go to when you get home. Make lots of new friends.'

'Yeah, I will,' Ben agreed, playfully punching Greg on the arm.

'What did they give you?' Dan asked as they drove home. Ben opened his gift. It was a Bible and practically everyone in the church had signed it. As Ben flicked through its pages he came across a verse that had been underlined.

They that wait on the Lord will renew their strength. They will rise up on wings like eagles, they will run and not grow weary. They will walk and not grow faint.

'So that's why they call themselves the Eagles,' Ben said out loud.

'Ben,' said his mother carefully, 'when we get home would you tell me your story all over again. I'd like to get it on tape and maybe write a book about it.'

'Yes, Claire, that's an excellent idea,' Dan enthused.

Ben agreed. 'Oh and Mum, I know just the title for it. You could call it, *Slam Dunk into Reality.*'

Claire mused over this for a while. 'Slam Dunk into Reality,' she said quietly. 'I think I like that.'

TRAIL BLAZERS

This is real life made as exciting as fiction! Anyone of these trailblazer titles will take you into a world that you have never dreamed of. Have you ever wondered what it would it be like to be a hero or heroine? What would it be like to really stand out for your convictions? Meet William Wilberforce who fought to bring freedom to millions of slaves. Richard Wurmbrand survived imprisonment and torture. Corrie Ten Boom rescued many Jews from the Nazis by hiding them in a secret room! Amazing people with amazing stories!

This is a series worth collecting!

A Voice in the Dark: Richard Wurmbrand

The Watchmaker's Daughter: Corrie Ten Boom

The Freedom Fighter: William Wilberforce

From Wales to Westminster: Martin Lloyd-Jones.

The Storyteller: C.S. Lewis

An Adventure Begins: Hudson Taylor

The Children's Champion: George Müller

CHRISTIAN FOCUS

Good books with the real message of hope!

Christian Focus Publications publishes biblically-accurate books for adults and children.

If you are looking for quality bible teaching for children then we have a wide and excellent range of bible story books - from board books to teenage fiction, we have it covered.

You can also try our new Bible teaching Syllabus for 3-9 year olds and teaching materials for pre-school children.

These children's books are bright, fun and full of biblical truth, an ideal way to help children discover Jesus Christ for themselves. Our aim is to help children find out about God and get them enthusiastic about reading the Bible, now and later in their life.

**Find us at our web page:
www.christianfocus.com**